PARABLES, FA

'Malachi McIntosh
extremes of our imagination and at the center of our
experience. The parables are visceral and unsettling,
beautiful and charming, all at once. Every character
stands out as much as they are a stand-in for a
stereotype; their chatty bonhomie is captured with
absolute finesse. This book is a delightful read...'
Meena Kandasamy

OTHER TITLES FROM THE EMMA PRESS

SHORT STORIES AND ESSAYS

Blood & Cord: Writers on Early Parenthood, edited by Abi Curtis
How Kyoto Breaks Your Heart, by Florentyna Leow
Night-time Stories, edited by Yen-Yen-Lu
Tiny Moons: A year of eating in Shanghai, by Nina Mingya Powles

POETRY COLLECTIONS

Europe, Love Me Back, by Rakhshan Rizwan

POETRY AND ART SQUARES

The Strange Egg, by Kirstie Millar, illus. by Hannah Mumby
The Fox's Wedding, by Rebecca Hurst, illus. by Reena Makwana
Pilgrim, by Lisabelle Tay, illustrated by Reena Makwana
One day at the Taiwan Land Bank Dinosaur Museum,
    by Elīna Eihmane

POETRY PAMPHLETS

Accessioning, by Charlotte Wetton
Ovarium, by Joanna Ingham
The Bell Tower, by Pamela Crowe
Milk Snake, by Toby Buckley

BOOKS FOR CHILDREN

Balam and Lluvia's House, by Julio Serrano Echeverría, tr. from
    Spanish by Lawrence Schimel, illus. by Yolanda Mosquera
Na Willa and the House in the Alley, by Reda Gaudiamo,
    translated from Indonesian by Ikhda Ayuning Maharsi
    Degoul and Kate Wakeling, illustrated by Cecillia Hidayat
We Are A Circus, by Nasta, illustrated by Rosie Fencott
Oskar and the Things, by Andrus Kivirähk, illustrated by
    Anne Pikkov, translated from Estonian by Adam Cullen
Cloud Soup, by Kate Wakeling, illustrated by Elīna Brasliņa

PARABLES

FABLES

NIGHTMARES

STORIES BY
MALACHI MCINTOSH

THE EMMA PRESS

for Miles

THE EMMA PRESS

First published in the UK in 2023 by The Emma Press Ltd.

Text © Malachi McIntosh 2023.
Cover design © Mark Andrew Webber 2023.
Edited by Emma Dai'an Wright.

ISBN 978-1-915628-19-0

A CIP catalogue record of this book
is available from the British Library.

Printed and bound in the UK by TJ Books, Padstow.

The Emma Press
theemmapress.com
hello@theemmapress.com
Birmingham, UK

There is little like knowing

I am an orchestra –
only rehearsing

– Victoria Adukwei Bulley,
'What it Means', *Quiet* (2022)

She arrives late at Bank station when the man decides to jump. She's meant to meet Matthew at the Tate Modern for their second date. So far, she's been lukewarm on him – but this time she has more hope, wants to rush home, change; gets waylaid at work running through, yet again, her PowerPoint presentation for Department Day, and hits the platform as the train comes in and the man next to her is gone.

Just gone. No leap or run or scream. No sign or sound except the sound. Just gone, like he never was.

And it takes the commotion of everyone else to even realise that it's even happened at all.

When she leaves the station it's with bodies in procession. Everyone with their phones out waiting for the first few bars of signal, then calling and texting, the tannoy apologising for *The delay to your journey*, Underground staff out and redirecting and enough people complaining about the hassle that it almost – doesn't – counterbalance the look on the faces of the people who saw.

But she didn't see. She stands out in the street as it was, in the city as it was.

She was right there next to him, standing there right next to him, but she didn't see.

Matthew texts her as she walks nowhere, rings her when the time for them to meet comes and goes and she's done three laps of an anonymous block and she answers finally and tells him A man He jumped And I saw it, even though she didn't see.

She didn't see.

And from then on whenever she talks about it – and she develops a special way to move into it, the story, to precede it, a kind of half-laugh that's not a laugh at all to end it – she'll make a face and pause and say, 'You know once,' and say she saw it when she didn't see.

She didn't see.

She always says that she did, and she never knows why she does. But she does it anyway.

I

Examination

They slept together in the same bedroom, but no longer shared the same bed. She'd told him over a year ago that it wasn't appropriate (her word, 'appropriate'), and bought him a camp bed, just to start, and wedged it against the far wall. The arrival of the bed meant the loss of the bookcase from the bedroom, the books now stacked, alphabetically, underneath where he slept.

They tended to wake up at the same time, her alarm clock bleating to them both, prodding each body up and out as it echoed. In summer the noise rang with sunlight; in winter the sound into the dark. Today it was set earlier than always, because today was today: the test.

The boy lay awake. His eyes opened about an hour before they were supposed to, found the ceiling and rolled into his eyelids as he started doing his sums. He began with the easy ones – the ones he knew he knew – then moved upwards into big numbers: three digits, four. He did as she taught him, checked his answers with subtraction, did everything twice, but then he got stuck, as always – he always got stuck.

He looked down, then, across at her sleeping, over the distance from his bed to hers. In the first weeks of lying alone he would, inevitably, wake up in the dark and suddenly feel cold, feel the idea sliming out of him that she'd decided to run away. He'd look across and in those first weeks, months, panic and throw off his sheets to see her, sneak the few steps to her blanket and burrow in. She'd stir and mumble and move her hands, but if he pulled his knees into his chest and stayed silent, breathed even, he knew he'd spend the evening in her heat, with her smell.

'Are you awake?' she said to him now.

'No,' he said, eyes open. 'Not yet.'

She made a noise, a yawn, slid up and back to rest on her forearms in bed.

'Can you boil some water for some tea?'

'Can I make the tea?'

'Just the water.'

She breathed another noise, a sigh or a yawn.

'You make it too weak. I have to teach you.'

She yawned again, sat her back fully against the headboard, her arms up then out – stretched – her face twisted up, and then her face at rest.

'Do we have to go?' the boy said.

Her arms slumped into her lap.

'I'm so tired. I don't know why I'm so tired.'

'Mom?'

'Of course.'

'Of course what?'

'Of course we have to go.'

'Why?'

'Because we do.' Her hands smoothed down her face, back through her hair – her hair everywhere. 'Because they all think you're something that you're not. And because of that they think we're something we're not. And we're going to show them.'

'I don't want to show them.'

She looked at him, yawned something he couldn't understand. And then the alarm went off.

*

The subway. Every week it felt like a million miles into and out of the city: the walk to the subway, the walk to the apartment, the walk up the stairs.

She'd met with his teachers so many times in the last two years it had turned into a second commute. Home. Smear a sandwich. Check the answering machine. Feed him, then drag him back to the bus, to the school. First, the tight smiles. Small talk – your trip – *oh really* – your work – *i have a cousin who* – coffee? – *oh tea? i'm not sure we have tea* – Then the warmup – *we think your son is very capable* – then business.

Eventually even they felt the routine was too routine and wanted to break it, to cut to the chase – they'd say that, 'I want to cut to the chase', gesturing with clenched fingers, now presenting themselves as no-nonsense, frank – people who spoke the truth and expected it back.

All the approaches aimed anyway at the same destination: whether they claimed to think he was capable or not, what they wanted, why she was there, was for them to tell her the myriad ways that he'd failed. Every time she met them, eventually, a white paper of red lines, a quotation from a parent of another child, his own admission, 'yes'. He was variously inattentive, disruptive, unsettled, troublesome, agitated, over-excited, rambunctious, too vocal, undermotivated, uninterested, volatile and, once, dangerous.

'Dangerous?'

'I don't say that very often,' the woman said, tapping her pen on the desk between them. 'But that's the best word for the way he behaves.'

She would be called in to discuss his report cards, to discuss his 'harassment' of girls his age, his refusal to stay in his chair, the wide eyes he directed everywhere except at the blackboard. She'd be asked what he watched on television, where he was in the few hours before she arrived back home from work; they'd question – ever so tentatively – where his father was – *he's nine now*, they said most recently, softly, *and for a boy his age it's very important.*

She'd nod at them. Take him home, scream at him. Sit him down with his schoolbooks on the kitchen table, just the two of them under the single bulb, teach him. Take him back the next week – walk bus walk – see the same old homeless man on a cart begging for change, the kids on Walkmans with skateboards, other women with their sons on bus seats reading thick books opened up on their laps. Him and her.

*

They ate breakfast together, her leg bouncing underneath the table out of sight.

'Can you do two times ten?' she said.

'Twenty.'

'Good. Ten times two?'

5

He paused, smiled. 'It's the same.'

'Four hundred twelve. Plus. Nine hundred and sixty.'

His eyes stared at some point beyond her body, his mouth slowly sliding open.

'Two. Seven.' He used his fingers. 'Thirteen. One three seven two?'

'Say it properly.'

'One thousand three hundred and seventy-two?'

She paused and counted on her own fingers. 'Good.' She nodded.

He nodded too, grinned, spooned cereal and chewed.

'They're going to ask you a lot of questions like that. Most of them will be harder.'

'I know.'

'Some will be really, really hard and they'll all be looking at you, maybe more than one person, but you have to do all of them, even the hardest ones. Okay?'

'Okay.'

'Are you scared?'

'A little bit.'

'Me too.'

*

He'd been expelled. Another problem with a girl, this time in his Thursday lunch. The story, as they told it, was that he had placed his hand, palm upward, on the bench where she was about to sit. When she was almost seated he grabbed her, she jumped and spilled her lunch and drink all over her dress. He laughed at her, covered in food slush, and she slapped him in the face.

Three adults in the principal's office. The boy at home. She'd come in to the principal's message on the answering machine, rang back to confirm, tonight, boiled spaghetti for her son, headed out of the house alone, only twenty-five minutes after she got in.

'You all work so late,' she said when she arrived.

All they did was stir.

She said nothing to the boy that night when she returned besides what was necessary: Turn it off, Brush your teeth. In the morning she waited until after he was dressed to tell him he wasn't allowed at school anymore. She asked him if he knew why and he squirmed and said 'no'. That set her off. She grabbed his t-shirt and shook him, asked him again and he said 'no', welling up. She left their bedroom, grabbed her slipper, grabbed him again and smacked him on his legs and his back and his head until her arm went numb. She left him crying on the kitchen floor. Sat on the floor of her room, cried too.

The principal tried to be nice, brought her coffee, sent his assistant or administrator, one of the ones she'd already met, to fetch it. *Well*, he said, *I'm sorry, but we've had enough.* He tried to be nice, said the best option might be a special school, mainstream education might be too much, and offered her tissues. He didn't say anything about the boy's father, but did, on exit, ask: 'Are you working right now?'

*

Think the two of them, walking to the subway, the boy's hand inside his mother's hand. A cityscape of uncollected trash bags and low buildings, more kids on skateboards. The boy walking beside her to the bus, practicing sums, trying analogies like *man is to arm as bird is to _____; up is to down as left is to_____; past is to future as now is to _____.*

They reach the subway and she pays for tokens, the boy watching her face.

'What are you looking at?'

'You.'

'Mind your business,' she says.

'I am.'

She smiles. 'Are you nervous?'

'Yes.'

'Don't be nervous. You're ready. What's the capital of New York?'

'Albany.'

'See? Good.'

'But I'm scared.'

She frowns, chews the inside of her bottom lip and walks with him down to the platform. Three trains come for the opposite direction before their train pulls in. They find seats, sit, the subway car empty, rattling, advertisements. The train makes its way, first above ground and all the rooftops, then into the tunnels.

A long pause. Then she says, 'Don't be.'

*

They emerged together from the subway into cold sunshine, tired after changing trains twice. She'd asked them if there was anywhere closer, but the people who called her said no, there were only a few test centres, only one open on weekends.

The city already awake, cars thinner than they would be in an hour. She asked at a corner store for directions to the school, the man behind the counter re-directing the question to his friend stocking the shelves, the friend saying he thought he knew where it was but didn't *know know for sure.* They wandered on, slightly lost, the boy gawping around, as always, the pressure of her hand on his too tight.

She tried to relax herself, tracing her way using the store man's suggestions along her old map now separating along its folds. She remembered arriving in the city with it, her stomach twirling, tracing her way to her first job. She remembered holding him on just her forearm when he was born, how little he weighed… bit her lip and then led her son, hard, tugged him hard when he lagged behind or got distracted, both of them breathing too shallow, walking faster as she checked and re-checked her watch.

They found a school building several streets away from where they had emerged from the train.

She tugged him. 'Come on.'

The inside of the school was better decorated than any he'd ever attended. The lobby curved a round, open oval, a wide staircase directly in front, hallways branching out of the long sides. Kids' work framed on all the walls, the school's name painted above the staircase and clean.

'It's empty.' She dropped his hand. 'Is this it? Is this where we're supposed to be? Does this look right? No one's here.'

She checked the address she'd written on the back of an envelope and looked around for confirmation, checked her map, dug through her handbag looking for change for a phone.

'This can't be the place,' she said, then looked at him. He didn't know.

Just as she turned toward the door and took his hand again, an old woman appeared, dressed in a beige skirt, beige cardigan, white shirt, making her way slowly down one of the long corridors holding a jug of water and a stack of cups. She smiled, the old lady, and apologised.

*

They sat together outside a classroom now on two plastic chairs dragged flat against a wall. There were people in the room they couldn't see, whose words they could almost hear, the assessors (the old woman's word, 'assessors'), and it would take them a short time to set up.

The boy tried to practice problems but everything fizzed like static in his head, his heart beating hard in the base of his neck. He looked up at his mother but it didn't help. He knew her faces. He knew the transitions from one mood to another, knew her moods, sometimes, even before they arrived. She was upset. Trouble twisted all around her mouth, her eyebrows pulled together and clenched in the centre of her head. He wanted to ask her if they were late but knew he shouldn't, even though he still wanted to.

They waited there together, the boy and his mother: his face aimed upward at hers; her hands pressed flat and tight between her knees, her head down, eyes closed, a position he had seen in others and taken himself while waiting for teachers, for students to apologise to, for the principal, for his mother to finish on the phone.

'We're going to take a test,' she'd said to him a month before. 'They want to see if you need to go to a special school, but you don't. You don't. You need the best. And we're going to show them.'

The Ladder

I'm telling you this story not because I believe it – I'm not sure that I do, really – but because when I heard it I felt like I had to tell somebody, and the best person I could think of to tell it to was you.

The guy I heard it from originally wasn't, to be honest, the most trustworthy guy I've ever met. A work contact, ex-football player type, huge neck like a normal guy's thigh muscle, like literally enormous – wore shirts that always seemed like they were about to explode. He always had a few choice details in his stories that felt… embellished, to put it mildly. But he swore by it.

'*Bullshit*,' I said to him when he finished. 'There's no way it happened like that.'

'It did,' said my friend. 'Word for word.'

'But how did they—?'

'It did,' said my friend. 'I swear on my mother's life,' he said, which he never did, with a look so serious I thought, *For real?*

'But I don't get it. What were they trying to achieve?'

He opened his hands, closed them. 'Same as everybody, I guess.'

*

The story is that there's this kid, Aaron, I don't remember his last name, something Polish, and he's a hotshot. He comes up out of some no-name school in Florida, applies to his first firm after graduation, just to try his luck, and they try their luck with him, say *Fuck it* and make him an offer.

He moves up to New York, starts at the firm, and he just takes to the work in a way that nobody expected. He's dynamite. But the first time they see him?

They do one of those three-week intensive training courses, all inclusive, that all the big firms were doing before the virus. Kids from all over the country flown in; kids from all over the world. The whole thing is that they're getting inducted into the company and the culture, learning the ropes, but the kids are also getting sized up every time they take a breath, go to the toilet to take a shit. It's cut-throat. Nobody fails training, as such, but it's not rare a guy disappears two weeks after they're done, culled.

When I say there are kids there from all over the place I don't mean everywhere, obviously. I mean the very best, the kids from the Ivys, the elite places in Europe, South America. Because of that, the training looks, on the first day, like a re-enactment of the J.Crew catalogue: even the ugliest guy there looks like he's spent the whole morning doing chin-ups and box jumps, except maybe for a half-hour break when he went to the tailor and a salon.

But then you've got our hero. He arrives in this over-sized brown blazer and sloppy grey khakis – you know, the type with extra fabric pouring onto the shoes and stuff, like he's Michael Jordan in the '90s; wears a floral tie, just looks ridiculous. In a room full, basically, of Adonises, you've got this kid dressed like the difference between the way a clown dresses and a normal guy. That first day everybody's staring at everybody else wondering where they found this loser, wondering if he's some kind of gag or activity for the training session. At lunch they're all ordering arugula salads and he's like *'Oh Jeez, no McDonald's?'*, and folks are feeling embarrassed for him.

But he's got a spark; they see it as soon as they start working together. The whole set-up is competitive: the new hires are broken up into teams, given tasks, time limits; there's a leaderboard. The whole company is organised on what they call 'the Ladder' – that is, as soon as you get in you're given a rank, and you know it and everybody else knows it. You're 0, and you've got to climb up. All through your time at the firm you're climbing, getting scores, moving on: in performance reviews you get your rank on the Ladder; after projects you get your rank on the Ladder. It stops being public after training but, no surprise, everyone's trying not to be the bottom guy; they all want the top, but nobody can top Aaron.

It's mostly shameless. Guys are doing the showy thing – trying to make small talk with the managers in the coffee breaks, flexing on each other about what they achieved in college and how hot their girlfriend is, but Aaron's quiet, barely talks, but as soon as the competitions start, he kills it. He's just a winner – knows how to get what he needs from his team, collaborates, makes way when necessary, pushes on when it's not; he draws people in, he lifts the team up – and, and this never happens, my friend says, his team wins every single thing.

They love it; he makes them all look great, but everyone else is kind of stunned. *This guy?* Aaron doesn't do *hey-look-at-me* victory parades like some of the peacocks on his team, but everyone working with him knows who's carrying them, and the managers on site wander over and watch and clock it too: this kid's special.

When training's done and they start working it's pretty much the same: he's still dressed like he borrowed his dad's wardrobe, but everything else is solid and the clients just snap to him. My friend says it's because he's not as intimidating as Brodie or Pericles from Yale. The other guys at the firm, they're scary: smart as hell, confident, smell like what your next paycheque looks like in your bank account. They've all already got connections and are just biding their time until they go into politics or run Dad's company or start yatching or whatever and it's no secret: you know and they know that they're going to rule the world. But Aaron? He's got this Southern drawl, he's got your phone from three years ago, and you and him watch the same TV shows. The other guys show up on site for a restructure and people are shitting themselves as soon as they open the door. If you're an employee at that place you know they couldn't give a fuck if you lived or died. But then you've got Aaron. He's still behind people getting fired left and right, don't get me wrong, but seeing him come in behind the other guys feels almost refreshing; people look at him and they feel like they've got a shot.

So they love him, the girls especially – the receptionists, the HR old ladies. He makes them go crazy.

They tell him trivial stuff about their lives, just off-hand drops about, you know, tough weekend because the kids were acting up, and he remembers the kids' names for next time. The other guys, the girls are interested in them too, of course, they're not blind, but they feel bad about it; Aaron – the smile, the twinkle in his eye, those deep nods when they tell him about their weekend plans or ask him if they should get more coffee for the room or something – he feels good to like.

And he builds on it. In the beginning he works hard – first one in, last one out. He drops the droopy wardrobe but keeps the charm, and six, eight, ten months in, my friend says, this guy is a force of nature:

'This manager recommends him – specifically him – for a big corporate strategy project when nobody else on the thing has less than three years' experience; he's blowing through the work, impressing the partners, is just jumping straight from project to project to project; PAs are literally fainting when he walks into the room, creaming themselves. A year later, not a single guy from his intake is anywhere close...'

But there's what you do and who you are. This kid Aaron, he doesn't like to talk about where he comes from, brushes questions aside when it comes up, changes the subject. The other guys are constantly telling their backstories. But Aaron never once mentions his family, doesn't let anything slip. He'll say something about the college he went to, but in a way that shows he's partly ashamed by it. It's a chink in him, and not the only one.

Mostly these guys finish a job and within an hour they're all wasted. Everybody's always out for drinks – birthdays: drinks; new hires: drinks; between assignments: drinks. You get to know your managers over drinks; you talk about the workday over drinks. Your whole life is working and last call. Christmas parties, training-day parties, strip clubs… But Aaron's on the edge of it. He's there drinking with them but is never once drunk; participates but never fully lets go. Now, he does stay out all night; you have to. He does jump in on the jokes, grabs his shot glass to toast whatever the hell they're toasting in that moment – but somehow the alcohol doesn't touch him; he's always in control. Twenty-three-year-old kid now, lives in Manhattan, is making wild money, but not once is this kid wasted in public. Holds himself like a rod.

'And that's nuts,' said my friend.

It is.

And guys start to catch on. Whether he's on site

or in the bar, he's still working – and that's not how it's supposed to be.

Eventually they're in some city, say Cleveland, on a job. The baseball team there is so shitty that one of the guys gets them all tickets for close to nothing and they all roll out to a game midweek.

They're up in the stands, good seats of course, about seven or eight of them together. It's baseball, so nothing's happening, and in the sixth inning one of the guys asks Aaron, pretty straight, 'Hey. Your family still around?'

And Aaron says, 'Sort of.'

The guy's hanging – 'sort of' isn't good enough and he's got time to waste. Aaron's cornered. It's a baseball game: he can't just fade back into the noise or the crowd like at a bar. The only sounds are the whiff of pitches into the catcher's glove; the only people moving around are buying hot dogs, stretching, falling asleep in their seats. He's got to give more. And he can read people – that's his talent; he knows he's got to give more. But he just sits there.

'What do you mean, sort of?'

'My parents've passed, but I've got a sister,' he says, and then obviously wants out of the conversation.

'Oh yeah? Older or younger?'

'Excuse me?'

'Your sister. She older or younger?'

'Yeah, younger.'

'What, like a teenager?'

'Twenty.'

'She back in—'

'No, New York,' says Aaron in a way that means, *Alright, dude, I'm good.*

'She hot?'

'What?'

'Your sister. She hot?'

If you've got eyes you can see that Aaron's somewhere he doesn't want to be. So this guy sees it too, of course. And Aaron? Here's this kid they're all starting to admire, but what's he hiding?

They're at a baseball game. There's been turnover since Aaron started – say 40% of the guys he works with now are new, have no stakes in him, see him as the establishment; he's senior to them. But this guy, the one talking to him right now, he's been there from the start, got the job at the same time, same intake, and yeah he likes this kid, but his parents paid as much as Aaron's whole neighbourhood probably cost to send him to school and one day Aaron's going to be his boss. And that's – what the fuck is that? Sure, this guy talking's not going to stay at the firm forever – he's got wider prospects, but still. Still.

'She hot?'

'You wish,' Aaron says, and tries to do it like he's in on the joke, but he's not.

'Based on the drought I'm in,' says the guy, 'I'd take anything. I bet she's hot.'

"Cause I am?"

'Nah, because you're being such a bitch about it. When do we meet her?'

There's literally panic on Aaron's face now and he knows the other guy's watching. As a result, for the first time since he's been at the firm, he gets something totally, completely wrong.

'Yeah. I'm pretty sure nobody wants you to do that,' he says.

Then crack.

Everybody's out of their seats. The ball skimming the skyline, out of the stadium. A home run.

The crowd goes wild.

*

So, who's the sister?

I asked my friend that and he said, 'That's it. That's

the question everybody's thinking about now. Who's the sister, why doesn't he want us to meet the sister? And of course he doesn't want us to meet his sister. Who wants the guys at work to meet their sister? But at the same time, like the guy at baseball's thinking, what the hell is he trying to hide?'

You can see how this all picks up. My friend arrives at the firm when it all gets started. Week one he says he's learning how to log into his email; week two he's talking about the sister: *Who's the sister? Who's the sister?* They're making jokes: 'Is she a fatty, is that it?' But they're also thinking about why he didn't just bite back with 'When I meet yours' or 'The best you can do is my little sister?', or anything – anything other than telling the other guy that he can't. Because of course he can. This guy can do whatever the fuck he wants.

Independently of each other, they start springing it on him. At a bar, a guy that Aaron doesn't realise knew about what happened at the game says, 'Hey, your sister. She's here in the city, why not bring her out?' In an elevator on the way up to a meeting a guy says, 'Family's the worst, right?' – letting it float there, giving Aaron space to do something with it. Stuff like this is happening every few days and every time

Aaron closes it down or ignores it but you can only do that so much –

They're at another bar. Their regular ritual: job's done, get hammered. Aaron goes up to get drinks but he's totally sober, as usual, gets to talking to two girls. You have to see this kid now: crisp shirt, beautiful suit, eyes glowing in the light. It's downtown New York so everyone there is gorgeous – you know, the kind of people that when you see them you kind of catch your breath; you don't know what to do; you don't want to turn back to check them out but you've got to – you know this is the one and only time you'll ever see someone like that so you can't resist. And Aaron now? He's at home in this.

A guy comes over, claps him on the shoulder, but then when he sees these girls – and these girls are special – he does bug eyes and says, 'Oh shit I thought you were talking to your sister.' It's playground stuff and, like at the game, the kid's reaction should be to shrug it off, but he can't; he just can't do it.

He shoves the guy to the ground. The girls were having a good time before but they go cold – the whole room feels things get weird. A second later, girls have gone. Volume's dropped. Space has cleared. Like the two guys are in some pocket, a cocoon.

'*What the fuck?!*' says the guy, scrambling to stand up.

Every minute and every second of every day you've ever seen this kid it's like he's in the ballet or something, holding himself rigid, keeping his words correct, and now it's gone and he sounds like the kid you'd expect him to be – up from the country, a nobody. He looks like the others except now his blazer's slipped, his nose is flared. '*What is this?*' he says.

'It's a fucking joke.'

'*It's not funny,*' he says, and the other guys have gathered.

He's surrounded now. He's looking around. Maybe he's panting.

But he's got no move.

Nothing.

He apologises. Says he's had too much, but nobody's dumb. It's Aaron: he hasn't. He buys the round he was buying. Stays at the table long enough for the pinch of it all fade. Then he slips away.

Word travels. *He did what? Holy shit. Where?*

Two things I should say now is that I keep saying 'guys' when I talk about the firm like it was only all men. It wasn't. There were some women, maybe a few gay guys, but they didn't really last that long. They were there but they weren't there, just passing through. You've probably heard of some of them – went on to great things after they left; on the same path as the rest – dad's firm, D.C. Kept their heads down, did what they had to.

The other thing is that nobody hated this kid. The opposite. He was clearly the best of them, hands down. And every day he was putting money into everybody's pockets while still being humble. He doesn't get drunk? Well, maybe he's Christian, or he's got a crazy-high tolerance, some guys do. The clients all want to bone him? Well, he works like a demon; he's pulled everybody out of a few scrapes and that makes it easier on that front for everybody else. He's a dedicated guy, nice; but still, did he ever really fit in?

Word travels. Everybody's going crazy about it. They have theories, including, my friend said, that the sister is Hillary Clinton, which is a great one. ('I'd hide it too,' I told him.)

And they all decide without ever agreeing it: they've got to find her.

There are two guys at the place who've been there for years. They love the job – the travel, the salaries, the whole culture. I think one is married and the other is single – either way, no kids between them, plenty of time. Both are pretty secure in what they're doing, have solid places on the Ladder, don't need to prove anything to anybody; don't really need the money.

One of these guys, let's call him Erik, decides he's going to solve the mystery – he's going to find this girl, whoever she is. New York is big but it's not that big. He's an analyst; he makes six figures, can drill through a profit and loss and see what the numbers are hiding in about six minutes. It's just some twenty-year-old girl.

He's straight onto the apps. Aaron's not on anything, which they should have already clocked as suspicious, but he went to this college – so Erik finds the college; he knows Aaron's age so he knows his graduating class, finds the kids from the class who don't have their profiles private. He knows Aaron went to the college closest to home – they got that out of him, at least – so he works out the high school he probably went to, or at least a ballpark, and finds about a hundred people who could be classmates, then which ones of them know a girl with the same last name, or have younger brothers or sisters who know a girl with the same last name—

Gotcha.

Taryn ——, profile marked as private, location New York.

He switches apps. Private on the one, but public on the other in grids and grids of pictures.

Nothing exciting. No wild revelations. Just a girl, looks about eighteen, at most, and it's her with her friends, her in a bikini on a beach, her with some guy, then with a different guy lower down, pictures of her food. She's one of these girls with small tattoos all over the place and there are a couple of shots of her getting inked, a lot of skin.

Erik's a little thrilled when he's doing the detective work, clicking through, feeling like a hero the closer he gets to the answer, nearer the secret, but then when he actually finds her the excitement just stops. It's just some girl. Could be anybody's sister.

In more than one of the new pictures there's this bar where the girl works, some Brooklyn dive; it's tagged. He calls the other guy, we'll call him Devon, and tells him, 'Dude, I found her.' And he sells it hard – overegging the work he's done, how he located her. And then it comes to him:

'Let's go down there.'

'Why?'

'I don't know. Let's just go down there and see her.'

'Oh. Shit,' says Devon. 'You're twisted.'

'Why?'

'I know what you're thinking. You are fucking nuts.'

It's a week, two weeks later when Devon, Erik and Aaron are all on a job. It's a straightforward one – strategic review because stock has been pretty flat for a couple years; company wants to know how to supercharge, break into the big leagues and so on. Just a small team on it, about six of them. Company's given them a meeting room to camp out in and they're all in there on their laptops, each guy with a different part of the operation to review. This is all bread and butter to them; this is what they do week in and week out.

And they work quietly. Whatever they look like, all these guys came top of their class; they know how buckle down. All you hear in the room are keyboards clattering, bodies shifting in seats. They're wearing their jackets – this is back when people still wore ties; they're working. Maybe around this time in the day a guy might ask another guy where he's getting lunch and a third guy might say he'll come out for five but he's got to get through these spreadsheets.

Maybe Aaron's noticed that Erik and Devon are acting a little weird around him, keeping their distance, but it's been like that since Cleveland. He's probably just focused when Erik pipes up.

'I didn't tell you guys.' He's looking at his laptop, talking while he's typing. 'You ever been to place called Burn Bar?'

Aaron's a professional, doesn't flinch.

'Nah,' says whichever other one of them.

'Me and Devon went. Total shithole. Utter utter trash.'

'Why'd you go?'

'Just went dude,' says Devon. 'Slumming.'

'You guys need hobbies,' says another.

Aaron's not spoken, he's typing some report, no one's next to him and he's just typing and typing and typing, maybe even speeding up.

'It was *awful*, dude. *Awful*. People in there? You know how like after they flunk out of community college people want to come up here and make it? Like just being here sharing a room with ten people is cool because you can ride for two hours on the subway and be in the city? Like they think someone's going to see them bartending and, like, buy their craft beer company or whatever? Of the million of them, someone's gonna make them a *tattoo model* or some bullshit – and just like *overlook* the fact that they're trash?'

Most of the guys have checked out of the conversation by now. But Erik's only really talking to Aaron anyway; everyone else is just audience.

'Anyway, the place is full of no-hopers.'

'But the beer's cheap,' says Devon.

'Yeah. Everything's cheap. Beer's cheap. Girls are cheap… Staff are cheap.'

Aaron's stopped working now. Can't even pretend.

'Anyway, picked up the bartender,' says Erik, finally looking up, at Aaron.

'Was she hot?' says one of the other guys, to his screen.

'Nope.' He starts typing again. 'Total dog.'

'She dirty?'

Erik just smirks and Devon smiles wide. Both just keep on typing.

What does Aaron do? He doesn't know if the bartender Erik's talking about is his sister, although she must be. Does he jump up screaming? Does he undercut the guy, make a joke about him – say he's the dog? Does he get in on where the conversation goes because naturally now everybody's talking about girls they took home, their worst experiences, the ugliest ones, tag teams in college, does he respond? Does he say *No, be respectful?* Does he share a story? Does he have one?

Your whole face and body would be on fire. You'd want to be anywhere else, anywhere else in the world; it'd be like someone clamped a hand over your mouth, was pinching closed your nose.

Erik doesn't do the big reveal, doesn't hold his phone up and pass pictures of Aaron's sister around or anything and say *Hey Aaron, what do you think?* But it's clear it's a set-up, and that Devon's in on it. And they've got him.

They've got him.

'They've got him,' says my friend.

'But why?' I asked.

'Why do you think?'

They're on the job for the rest of that week and it's like the kid's half-dead. He's limp in the presentations to the clients; doesn't do his charm-attack on the secretaries – or he starts the week with one and then just abandons it. He's like a bag of empty skin. They do the end-of-the-job bar trip and he checks out from the beginning, says he can't go. Vanishes.

'And he calls his sister at some point and confirms?' I asked my friend.

'Who knows.'

'What do you mean, who knows? That's the whole story. Either the guy's got with his sister or he didn't. Why wouldn't the kid call? Say, *Hey what the fuck, what'd you do?*'

'Maybe he does call. What's he say?'

'He says, "You fucked some guy from my work or what?"'

'And she says, *None of your business.* Or she says, *Yeah I did.* Or she says, *What are you talking about?* Or, *Had a drink with a guy and woke up the next morning. He was sweet. I liked him. Never met him again.* What difference does it make? Who cares about the sister? They've got him. He's done.'

My friend says everything Aaron has that makes him special just unravels. He's messing up the numbers; he's not exciting the clients: from then on he's just not the same kid anymore – he's not way worse than anyone else, but he's not better, and that's not good enough. The other two, Erik and Devon, it looks like they don't tell anybody else about their little adventure; don't even make reference to it again. And as the seasons change the whole topic of who Aaron's sister is just dies away – some guys switch companies, people go on vacation. Some guy's getting married.

But the kid. One of the partners calls him in and says, 'What's happening? It's like we're losing you. We're concerned.'

The way Aaron's sitting it's like he's in the principal's office; he's in the new clothes but he's slumped in a way that they look all wrong. And he just says he's been having personal stuff, hasn't been sleeping.

The partner asks, 'What's on your mind? What's happening?'

And Aaron's looking at his knees for forever, then says, 'Can you tell me where I am? Where I stack up?'

It takes the partner a few beats to realise the kid's talking about the Ladder. The thing is that everyone can always check where they are on the Ladder. My friend says there's even an app they have now so it's always with you – although he can't remember if they had it back then.

Anyway: the kid should know this, must know this, but the partner's trying to help him, so he gets his computer out, looks him up, tells him his number. He's up there. He's not the highest. But he's right up there.

'So I did alright,' says Aaron. 'I guess.'

On the way out, at the end of that day, the partner slaps the kid's back, tells him everything will be fine. Everyone goes through slumps. That's the way it works. You fight back.

And Aaron doesn't turn up for work ever again.

*

I told my friend *Bullshit.*

'It's bullshit. So where's this kid now?'

'Aaron? Nobody knows.'

'What, he's dead now or something? He died from this?'

'No, you dickhead. Obviously none of that would've killed him. But yeah. Just vanished. *Poof.*'

'Like right off the face of the Earth?'

'Like here today, gone tomorrow. Wouldn't you?'

'And the sister?'

'Who cares about the sister?'

'But this kid's got so much promise. He just folds like that? That easy? Me, I'd fight back. I'd stick it out. There's no way I would—' but my friend was laughing, had started laughing. Laughing and laughing like I'd just told him the funniest joke in the world.

II

Limbs

The package arrived the same day that my girlfriend and I broke up. It came late, after hours of Emma trying to contact me – first texting in the morning to say that we should talk, then missed-calling me at lunch, then texting me again to say I needed to call her in the late afternoon, then missed-calling me during my Monday meeting with my line manager, then texting me I found someone else x, at the end of the day.

It was five-thirty and I rang her back but she didn't pick up. I rang again in five minutes and she said, on the phone finally, that it was exactly like me to ignore her calling until it was an emergency.

'But I was working,' I said.

'Mm,' was her response.

The rest of the conversation was Emma describing some guy she'd met out at her friend Steph's hen do, named Gary – of all things – at some club, who'd she let text her, and then met up with once for a drink and enjoyed it, and while she was speaking I was watching this new guy Ryan staring at the water cooler like he didn't understand how it worked.

I tried to gesture to him. 'Just press it, mate,' I said, then, 'I can change,' to Emma.

'Mm.'

'You don't think I can.'

'I don't know what I think. But I know I'm getting tired of thinking…'

I sat at the back on the top deck of the bus on the way home with my head against the glass. When I got in I saw that I had only a centimetre of ketchup, some carrots, and a sealed bag of dark wet rocket in the fridge, and a can of mushy peas in the cupboard.

'What a day,' I said, and the door knocked with the delivery.

I don't really remember the deliveryman's face, but he was young, I think, with frayed jean shorts on, work boots, and a company top. He had a hand trolley parked to his left, and on it, filling it, was a one-metre by one-metre wooden box.

I hadn't ordered anything, told him that, and he made me check the name.

It was mine.

'Where's it from?'

'No clue, mate.' He had a bit of an accent, possibly Polish. 'Sign here?'

'Don't you have some sort of manifest or something?' I said, taking the little Ghostbusters device that they carry around with them and scribbling into it.

He looked down at himself, at the left and right pockets of his shorts, behind his back, patted his thighs. 'No,' he said, genuinely. 'Don't think so.'

He wheeled in the crate, tipped it up off his trolley in the middle of my living room, and then wheeled himself out, pale calves in brown boots, waved goodbye and shut the door.

I had no idea what it was, walked around it but saw no clues. There wasn't much to it: about ten slats of some sort of light-coloured wood on each side, nailed together, box-shaped, with one of those cling film labels stuck to the top that I peeled off at the same time my phone vibrated in my pocket. A text, from my mate Andy:

pint?

'Must be from home,' I said aloud to the box, and texted back where r u?

finished work mate

Then another from him: bored.

There was no obvious way into the crate. I started thumbing another message into my phone and squatted, stroked the fingertips of my empty hand along the seams between the planks of wood, tried to slide my nails into the gaps. Nothing doing. I circled it in a squat, like a crab-man, pushing my fingers into the crevices until I realised that the top of it was separate from the rest, with nails driven into it vertically – some sort of lid.

I texted: just got a package from my mum i think

epic

hilarious, I wrote, Its massive. you could fit a – I stopped, thought, typed – giraffe – in it. I went to press send but then added Easily, and grinned, then sent it.

The screen said that Andy was writing but then the dialogue box disappeared.

I set my phone on top of the crate, went into my kitchen, my flat so small and open-plan that the kitchen was four steps away from where I was standing, opened a drawer, got a hammer, and took the four steps back. I held the hammer up, rotated it so the hook end faced the box, posed that way for a minute, thought *Oldboy*, then got three short texts from Andy:

pint?

Then

hour?

Then

the usual?

ok I wrote, tucked my phone into my front pocket and dug the hammer's back under the lid and wrenched, wrenched again – it was stuck tight – and creaked and creaked the lid up, bit by bit, until it came off.

Inside the crate, in various different lengths, thicknesses, and skin colours – from what looked like a range of different ages – were about thirty to forty severed limbs.

'*Fucking hell*,' I said. '*Jesus*,' and dropped the hammer.

I bent down and got the lid up and backed away, holding it to block my body, and checked the packing label again and it was definitely in my name, my address. I looked around my flat but there was nothing there to see, and Andy texted back:

katie's coming

'*Shit*,' I said.

Katie was a girl I'd fancied for over two years and I was positive that she'd started to feel the same way. A workmate of Andy's, she'd come out with us from time to time, could hold her drink – stuck to pints, ciders – had lovely grey-green eyes, perfect teeth, an American movie star's smile, clean skin. Emma was gone and I was single again. Work had been mental. I looked at the opened crate and thought about Katie – her smooth dark hair, the fact that she was into running, her nice hands, legs.

I went for the pint.

It was a good laugh, actually. I told them both when I arrived that Emma had dumped me and I got the standard sympathy – *Ah mate. How you taking it? There're more fish in the sea* – and got excused by Andy from buying the next round even though I'd arrived late and their pints were almost all foam. I hadn't mentioned Emma leaving me specifically as a signal to Katie, but saw in the way she gathered her hair and lifted it onto her shoulder, away from me, tilted her head and smiled her blockbuster smile, that she'd taken it that way.

'I'm sorry,' she said.

'It's alright. I could tell it was in the cards. We'd been growing apart a bit.'

'It's still not nice.'

'Nah, but it could be worse.'

Andy returned, pints held like a bouquet.

'Ah well,' he said. 'To freedom.'

'To freedom.'

Once the door of my flat had closed I'd turned back and thought I shouldn't leave the crate, but then

I decided an hour away from it wouldn't change anything; it might even help me to make sense of it all, and then I was in the bar and saw Katie – who looked amazing – and then the conversation started to flow and I fell into the moment. It was great banter. Katie was as she always was: quick-witted, sarcastic, sharp with a joke and much funnier than Emma. Andy too was on almost perfect form.

'Mate,' he said, mid-flow, mid-story, 'that whole night was bananas in pyjamas.'

I was only three pints in when I noticed that Katie was giving me all the signs: still playing with her hair; maintaining eye contact with me for ages, even when I wasn't talking; laughing at things I said that weren't that funny, far harder than they really deserved. I'd say something and she'd reach across the table and touch my hand like she was encouraging me, petting me.

'Arsenal, mate,' Andy said, breaking one long dose of Katie's grey eyes. 'Fuck. It's not even October yet and it's already like, Arsène mate.'

'I know.'

'It's just disgraceful. Like, fool me once,' he took a swig of his pint. 'You know? You just feel embarrassed at this stage. Like tormented. I just want to ring Wenger and say, mate...'

'Bon soir,' Katie said.

'Yeah,' Andy grinned, chuckled. 'Bon soir mate. What the fuck?'

We all laughed.

Emma and I had been together for just over a year which meant I was well out of practice. I started thinking that I should try to convert Katie's obvious interest into something else, but couldn't work out how to do it in a way that didn't feel awkward. Her hand on and off my hand was ongoing, there was constant contact between her knees and my knees under the table – but I was useless, and ended our evening with a 'We have to do this again', like a mug, rode the bus back like a doughnut and got back to my flat steaming and feeling annoyed.

It wasn't just my lack of skill with Katie – although that was a big part of it – it was also Emma, what happened finally hitting me on the slow walk up the stairs to my flat. I was alone. I was dumped for someone she met on holiday, on a hen do for God's sake, named Gary of all things, and I flicked on the main light in my flat and right in the middle of the floor was the crate, just like I'd left it.

I'd completely forgotten it was there.

I approached, hazy, half-drunk, my balance somewhere just off to my left and the room not quite spinning yet but not quite straight either. If not for the alcohol I don't think I would have had the courage to go back to the box and lift the lid a second time. But I had drank. Was a bit drunk.

Inside was like the meat section of your local supermarket but with the plastic ripped off the chicken, the ham, the liver, everything slid from its tray and poured into a cardboard box in the centre of the aisle. The fact that there were arms and legs in it was bad enough, but the rawness, the fresh fleshiness of it all hit me the hardest. Everything intertwined, overlapped, filled to the brim and, unlike earlier, with an almost metallic smell.

I closed it and coughed – coughing and hacking and hacking and hacking coughs up into my closed fist and out of my nose at the smell. With the lid on the stink of it pretty much vanished, but without it the rawness filled my mouth.

It was about midnight by then and I had work the next morning. I'd had quite a lot to drink, six rounds, and thought if I phoned anyone about this with the alcohol on my breath and my balance gone, in the state I was in – I don't know; I knew I'd have a better plan of action in the morning, when I was sober.

I started to brush my teeth with the crate reflected in my bathroom mirror, then closed the door. Went out afterwards toward my bedroom, the room rotating now, and had to pilot a way around the crate, paused and thought I ought to cover it up, out of respect, and fetched a sheet from my cupboard and laid it over on top and turned off the lights.

And overslept. I had one of those mornings where you feel like you're dreaming your alarm goes off, and snap up to see that either it never rang or you snoozed right through it.

I leapt from bed, a headache like a brick swapped for my brain, and dived into the shower, dressed, and left the covered crate, in its sheet, for the crush of the bus, a run down the street, the elevator and the office.

I didn't neglect it. At work I searched online for solutions between emails and meetings but didn't turn up much. The police were the obvious option of course, but I still wasn't clear on what to say to them and how I would frame things in a way that didn't feel suspicious, and I couldn't call them from work – or I could, but then they would probably come into work and I'd have to meet them in the office, my colleagues watching and wanting to know what was up. I'd need a story for my line manager, for everyone, and it was too difficult. I typed the non-emergency number into my phone anyway, for later, and checked other things. I searched for 'crate of limbs' online but regretted it as soon as I did, clicked away. I searched for 'people trafficking' to see if that could be some link, to see if there was a specific phone number for help or something, but was drowned in pages and pages on the topic and knew reading through all of it would take too long. I wasn't a detective, was on my work computer. I needed to keep it straightforward: I'd get home, call the police, they'd sort it out, and that would be the end of it. On the way back on the bus I could work out specifically what to say. Simples.

But then around three o'clock or so Janette, who had the desk to my right, passed an envelope heavy with pound coins to me, her telephone wedged into her shoulder. I opened it and inside was a card – *Sorry You're Leaving* – for Geoffrey, one of my older colleagues, who was moving to Australia. Almost everyone else had signed it.

'Shit,' I said to Lorraine, who sat on the desk to my left, leaning in towards her. 'Is it Geoffrey's thing tonight?'

She shook her head at me. 'Obviously.'

I checked my Outlook calendar and right there in it, at six, was Leaving Do.

'Oh no I don't know if I can come,' I said. 'I've got this – this other thing on, at home.' But even as I said it I knew I was stuck. Geoffrey was a nice guy, had done a lot for me over the years, gave me advice on how to manage my manager when I first arrived. He was a laugh, in general, around the office, always upbeat. 'Shit,' I said again to Lorraine. 'I completely forgot it was today.'

I had to go, and rolled out with everyone to a bar in the middle of town, about twenty minutes by bus from my flat. When we arrived, Geoffrey said he'd written a goodbye speech he wanted us all to hear but he waited ages to say it. Someone ordered chips, olives, we got a round in.

I want to say I spent the wait for Geoffrey's speech feeling anxious and checking the time, but I didn't. The handful of people on our team who usually rushed home to their kids were out with us. My line manager was out with us. The receptionist was out with us. We were all there and the mood was really good, really nice. By the time Geoffrey stood up to thank everyone, about half-seven or eight, and thanked me, personally, I didn't want to say goodbye but had to – did the rounds of hugs and handshakes, gave Geoffrey a massive pat on the back and bolted to the bus stop, where I got a text: what are you up to tonite?

It was an unknown number and I feared the worst, wrote back, who is this?

The dialogue bubble.

Gone.

There.

Gone.

Then: RUDE!

Then: KATIE!

It was already dark: the sort of time in September when the days are creeping shorter but it's still a bit warm. Above me the electronic counter in the bus shelter said I had a fifteen-minute wait. I checked the time now – about 8:00 or so – and made some rough calculations. I just couldn't do it.

not tonight mate, I wrote, busy, but didn't send it, stood up, paced inside the shelter trying to think of what I could add to take the sting out, to keep up what she was brave enough now to show, to not put her off. but how about tomorrow? what are your plans for this weekend? I thought maybe I ought to retype the whole thing and open it with a joke, like, bit keen? But no – I deleted it all, looked at our four messages above the empty response box. I really, really didn't want to put her off.

I wrote I could come for one? pressed send before

I could rethink it, and met her, Katie, just around the corner. We stayed for two, then three, and I spent the night at hers.

It was a surprise, but the opening details aren't really that exceptional: more touching, more eye contact, more open flirting. At about ten she invited me back to her flat for a cup of tea we both knew I didn't want or need, and I followed.

The rest was glorious. A bit sloppy, of course, but with that amazing feeling you get in those rare times you actually pull someone you really, really fancy and you finally touch, and see naked, all of the things you'd imagined to yourself. Katie there with me wiped Emma completely out of my mind. I thought at the start that I should have sorted out what was back at my flat, but I knew it would be waiting, and if I messed up with Katie she might not be.

'You have a nice leaving do?' she asked, grinning, after we woke up.

I cuddled closer, grinned back. 'Can't complain.'

'I'm jealous of Geoff,' she yawned, one of her legs winding itself tight around both of mine. 'I wish I was moving to Australia.'

'Put you off that quick?'

'No not like that!' she said and play-smacked my arm. 'I mean, it's like, it's a nice life. All that space. Everything's cheap.'

'Dunno, I've never been. I was supposed to go before I started uni but couldn't get a good flight. Went to Fiji instead. It was alright. Didn't get up to much.'

She shifted about a bit. 'I've got an old school friend out there. No one can afford to buy a flat here but she and her husband have got, like, a farm, three kids. They keep posting up these pictures—'

'I know,' I said. 'I've got a friend in New Zealand.'

'It's ridiculous, isn't it? I can barely save a deposit and she's like on a jetski the whole time.'

We separated slowly – talked for a bit longer about this and that until I had to go to work, do the walk of shame thing to a clothes shop, buy a shirt. I didn't get home until well after seven that night – the crate sitting there, draped, right in the middle of everything.

I sighed and lifted up the edge of the sheet and saw, in just over twenty-four hours, that the box's outside had somehow spotted with wide circles of grey and green mould. I dropped the corner back down, and took my phone out shaking my head.

I had to tackle it. Right, I thought, clicked through

to the non-emergency number and tried to rehearse some lines. As I went to call, I got a notification that Emma had sent me a message. I went to it but there was nothing in it – just a full stop.

'What does that mean?' I said.

Doesn't matter, I thought, went back to the emergency number, walked an orbit of the crate staring at it, but then went back to the message – a full stop? – then clicked into some photos of Emma and I together, smiling outside of various places, on our holidays. I realised I'd forgotten the name of the place in Malaysia we went, scrolled through emails to look it up, saw a friend had sent me a link to a video, in between all the junk mail, but I didn't watch it, put the phone down on my couch.

The thought bloomed that if Emma was there she'd know exactly what to do. Katie was fun but I still held something, some feeling, for Emma – of course I did – we'd barely broken up – and Emma was good at motivating me. This Gary guy, whoever he was, didn't deserve her. So I texted her back: Hey.

It wasn't the right thing to do. I knew it as soon as it went, even though describing it doesn't make any sense. The crate was there and I walked around it watching my phone's screen not responding, and felt ashamed – **Hey** shining in my face.

I put the phone down, leaned against the kitchen counter and stared at the crate. I walked to it, around it, then snatched the whole sheet off.

It was covered in mould. On the top, where the sheet was tightest, the blossoms had height, depth, texture, and again, I opened the lid.

I think I thought I needed to see it, to be able to describe it, to be reminded, to fix it in my mind. I also think I half-hoped somewhere inside that the problem would have resolved itself, that it all would have been transformed into a stack of jumpers from my mum or something, but it hadn't. Nothing was any better; it was the same thing it had been but worse, starting to rot. Fingers and feet. Long and short. Kids and adults. The smell.

I sealed it back up and draped the sheet.

I had to deal with it, I thought, sighed and sat on my couch and tried again to think about what I would say. I'd received this package yesterday. No, the day before. And I opened it and I saw all this. *Why did you wait so long to call us* they'd ask, and I'd say *I was actually really busy.*

'That's stupid,' I said out loud. No. I'd say I want-ed to read more about what it was, work out what it was about first before I did anything, but that didn't make any sense either.

I stood up and walked to my kitchen, to my fridge, and opened it, while still thinking, to the same rotting bag of rocket, carrots, few streaks of ketchup in a bottle. I felt hungry, checked the time, rang Katie.

I was avoiding it, to be honest, and Katie and I saw each other again that night, at her flat, and then the week exploded. We were a man down at work so it got even busier and then Emma texted me to say that her and her hen night fling Gary had already broken up, that she'd made a mistake – that she knew it as soon as she saw my message. I didn't really know how to react to that so just left it a few days and then she called me, bawling.

It was already Saturday. I was tired and felt like I needed some downtime, but couldn't just leave her somewhere crying alone and invited her round to my flat, pushing and straining the covered crate into the corner – putting a book on top of it, opened, like it was some sort of display or plinth.

Emma arrived with a bottle of wine and we talked. She was a good girl. She wasn't really funny or anything like Katie, but she was sweet, someone really caring, which you don't find that often anymore.

I was thinking that as she was telling the Gary story again and then I reached my hand across to her face, and she let me, and then I kissed her, opened her jacket, slipped off her shoes and socks.

The rest just happened, the old rhythms re-establishing themselves. We both knew each other well and although that made it feel step-by-step compared to Katie, that made it comfortable and easy too. Still, being there together with her on the couch, with the crate in the background, and then shifting into the bedroom – it felt wrong at the same time, made me realise how quickly I'd fallen for Katie, how the Gary thing had been a good way out.

In the morning I woke up slowly, then suddenly, to an empty bed, and an incredible, terrible smell, so thick and full that when I first realised I was smelling it, it made me retch.

I threw off the sheets, one hand over my nose and mouth and rushed out to Emma, standing in my living room in nothing, the book on my couch, the lid tilted up in her right hand, her left hand shielding her mouth, facing the crate, now completely covered in wet mould.

The stink of it was all I could breathe, feel, the stench almost physical on my skin.

I said, through my hand, 'Emma?'

She turned and I couldn't help but think how perfect her torso was, how beautiful her breasts were when they shook – her whole body. 'What the fuck is this?' she said, the contents of the crate now partly liquid, a slurry of brown, violet, of lumps and chunks.

'Someone sent it by mistake.'

'It's horrible,' she said, closed it. 'What is it?'

'I don't know. Just some kind of mess. Meat.'

'Meat? Why did you keep a box of meat? Send it back.'

'There's no address on it.'

'Then put it in the skip.'

'I think it's too heavy to carry down.'

'You can't keep it here, it's horrible. It's rotting meat.'

'No, I know,' I said. 'I wanted to—'

'Why would you keep this in your house?'

I took her hand, hugged her. 'No, I know. I'm sorry. I'll sort it out. Forget about it for now. Shhh,' I said, kissed the top of her head, tilted her chin and kissed her mouth, and knew when I did that it was the wrong thing to do.

She pushed me away. Stared for a minute – her body head to toe in front of me – all of her – shook her head. 'This was a mistake,' she said, stepping back, crossing her arms to cover her chest. 'I need to go home.' She turned for the bedroom.

'Emma,' I said, chasing her, watching her bend for, shake out, and slide on all her clothes. 'Sorry. I know that was patronising.'

'It's fine,' she said. 'It's what you do.'

'It's not.'

'Mm,' she said, buttoning her shirt, and then did something it's impossible to forget. She took the back of her hand, after she was dressed, and wiped her lips with it, scrubbing them on the space above her wrist, just behind her thumb, to get rid of me.

There's not much more left to say. I took Emma's leaving the way she did quite hard and got a bit depressed. Katie texted me at the start of the next week but I left it two days before getting back to her. When she replied I wrote something a bit evasive, said we should maybe meet up the following week. I went to the supermarket, finally, binge-watched a show everybody had been talking about, pulled a sickie and had a duvet day.

The crate stayed, covered, in the corner. I tried at first to follow what Emma had said, to lift it to put it in the bins outside, but I was right; it too heavy for me to do more than slide around by myself. And after over a week, with all the decay, there was no story I could believably tell the police about why I'd hadn't done anything about it. I checked the news to see if there were things happening that were connected but there weren't – there were some other things, but none of it was directly relevant—

So I left it. For another week, two weeks, the whole outside of it changing colour, the smell starting to leak. I bought some air fresheners and stuck them along the wall behind it and that largely did the trick. And then Katie and I started texting back and forth again but she was off on holiday, to Ibiza.

Jealous! I texted. When she came back I didn't see her.

A month, maybe more than a month after the crate arrived, Andy and I grabbed some pints and started talking with a group of girls, and two of them wanted to keep the party going after last call. I was the only one of the four of us who lived alone so, tins in hand, up the stairs, into my door and onto my couch, Andy pouring the beers into wine glasses for the girls for reasons all his own, and my cupboards, thankfully, stocked for a change. I put out some crisps and biscuits in bowls.

Andy laughed. 'Mate, what are we, six?'

My heart was racing and my mouth felt dry. It was like I was back at uni: two girls in my flat with my best mate. I slid on the couch next to the one I liked most, a redhead, and the other one, Andy's, pointed at a draped square thing in the corner of the room, a few books stacked on top of it, a half-drunk glass of beer on top of it, my house phone on top of it, my Xbox control.

'What's that?' she said.

'That what?'

'That box. What is that?' She pointed at it, then shifted her finger so it aimed at the bottom, where the sheet fell a bit short, and you could see a thin line of the wet mould, smiled awkwardly, shook her head.

'Oh that,' I said. 'Nothing. Just a box of severed limbs.'

Mirrors

He'd been on the M40 for a full hour when the sky broke open. It felt tropical, biblical: torrents slashing down from the heavens in an instant turned grey – sheets of rain fizzing his windscreen, unrelenting, barely disturbed by his wiper blades, and still another fifty miles to fucking Heathrow.

'Heathrow?' he'd said to Helen. 'From Manchester he could just jump on a train. From Birmingham he could just jump on a train. I could pick him up in twenty minutes from—'

'He didn't know.'

'But the name of where we live is *Birmingham*. It's called *Birmingham* International Airport. If I went to visit him in Washington I wouldn't fly into... I don't know, *Florida* Airport, would I?'

'Well, it's a comparatively small country. And I think it was the cheapest flight.'

'To Heathrow?' he said, but still lost, and then had to be the one dispatched to collect Sammy because he had the afternoon off.

And now standstill traffic. Rain like someone was dipping huge ladles into the sea and flinging them onto his Golf.

It was so easy to expect something else to go wrong: a flat tyre, the petrol light bright yellow, some kind of...

'Typical,' Henry said. Typical typical typical.

He'd never been good with families. Early girlfriends had credited it to him being an only child with only the barest parental oversight in his teens. More recently, at break-ups, it had been something about the fact that he'd never had a decent long-term relationship, that he had trouble not picking fights.

Helen, in particular, came from a background completely different, nuclear. She was the oldest of two children, raised in suburban Rhode Island, in a house like a house from an image search for 'house': lawn, fence, gates, etc.; trees astonishingly green. Her family was as stereotypically American as you could dream of, except they were Black; that fact the only disruption to what you'd expect them to be if you read about them on paper – her father a Black Republican, a Black Republican *donor*, something Henry couldn't imagine a real person being, even now, a year into Helen moving in with him, in the wake of at least

64

twenty transatlantic parental check-ins. Her brother Sammy was her father's understudy.

– Are you there yet? Helen said, her voice hollow in the car's speakers.

'No, the road's ridiculous. Standstill.'

– He's gonna be getting anxious. You know Sammy. I think he's landed already but I can't get a hold of him. He'll be freaking out.

'I'm a little at the mercy at the elements at the moment. Unless you know somewhere I can get a helicopter.'

It was a test, Sammy's trip – meeting family is always a test. Helen, in a way he'd never experienced or expected, had been pushing hard to take the relationship to the next level, something in no way helped by the fact that everyone else she knew seemed to be getting married, or pregnant, or both simultaneously. 'It's a life-stage thing,' his Jamaican friend Scissors had told him. 'Them get sweet; them get broody…'

– You should've left earlier. Why didn't you leave earlier?

'I had plenty of time.'

– Really?

Traffic was unmoving, unending, with no sirens or other signs of why, but at least the rain, now, was slackening off.

'I'm still waiting for someone to explain to me why he flew into Heathrow.'

– Yeah well, said Helen. Why'd you leave so late?

*

She'd arranged for her brother to visit them after negotiations that Henry felt only adjacent to, the decision made that Sammy would stay for a few days in the city before travelling down to London, then Paris, then Rome, and from there back home.

And Helen couldn't wait. She couldn't wait for Henry to finally meet her brother in person. Her brother was great.

Ahead loomed hours of stilted conversation about what Sammy was doing for work (Henry had no idea), what he was interested in (honestly, he had no idea), what he wanted to see… all the while watching Helen's face to check if he was passing the test.

And so, at Arrivals, so late he'd stopped calculating how late he was, journey-worn and cranky from the drive, he saw Sammy and was surprised. Not for anything to do with Sammy himself. He was, as far as Henry could tell, wearing something like the exact same thing he wore every day of his life – or his life so far as Helen's pictures had shown it: a baby-blue

Oxford shirt, baggy American-style pleated chinos, metal glasses, hair buzzed low. No, what surprised him was the other guy, standing next to Sammy with an identically sized overhead-compartment suit-case, its handle half extended, like Sammy's was, in a matching outfit of pressed chinos, Oxford shirt, shaved head, but no glasses. He was a White guy but otherwise identical, and Henry saw him and Sammy talking, animated, from a distance. It was uncanny: they were essentially twins but different colours – both within an inch of each other in height – five-foot something – grinning and chatting with all the same gestures.

Henry apologised: sorry for being late, traffic, rain.

'Oh it's cool, man. Don't worry about it. Total-ly happens,' said Sammy. 'By the way this is George right here.'

Sammy said they were travelling together, but if it was too complicated or too much hassle George could easily get a hotel.

'Yeah, easily,' George said, both of them with harsher American accents than Helen's years-sof-tened, work-softened near-Canadian. Both of them, still, Henry couldn't drop it, mirrors.

'Yeah. I can ask – or check with—' There was no point; Helen would, of course, say yes. 'I'm sure it's fine. And you two are... you're both... in college together?'

'Dude I finished college last year!' Sammy laughed.

'Dude!' said George. '*College*,' he laughed. 'Imagine if we were still in *college!?*'

'I'd die!' laughed Sammy.

'I'd beat you to it!' said George, with the same inflection.

'Yeah, of course,' said Henry, watching them.

He didn't probe any further about how they knew each other, because, to be honest, George was only slightly less a stranger than Sammy. Still, the two of them together felt increasingly bizarre. He walked with them to the car park, both following, suitcases rolling in sync, legs in sync, arms in sync, voices the same voice. They said all the things he'd expected Sammy to say – 'I can't believe I'm in London!' – 'Oh look. The cars are like *miniature*!' – but when doubled it made it less acceptable... more strange.

'Dude, when do we know if we need to mind the gap?'

'Mind the gap? What even is that? I think I've heard of it.'

'I don't actually even know. Should we ask Henry?'

'Yeah, let's ask Henry. Henry – what does it mean to mind the gap?'

When they got to the car George sat in the back, which made sense, but then Sammy joined him.

'I always sit in the back,' he said, as if that explained it – as if... what if there are only two of you in the car? But Henry just left it, allowed it; it's all a test, it's a test.

*

Within minutes, their conversation behind him became a rhythmic rise and fall of awe at things they must have talked about on their flight, simple things that seemed to fascinate them.

'Oh my god that English guy! He's got an umbrella!'

'George dude. Are you gonna eat like *all* the fish and chips on this trip or what? I'm gonna eat like *all* the fish and chips—'

'With sauce!'

'Do they do ketchup here, though? When my mom and me went to France before they were like *obsessed* with mayo.'

69

'All I really want to do here is Buckingham Palace. I want pictures of us just like *posed* in front of it for the 'gram.'

'Dude your Insta game is *so* weak. You *need* that content.'

Where Henry expected the blandest possible drive, he found himself glued to what they were saying – the emptiness of it, a kind of constant stream of nothing – and he felt a stronger and stronger urge to know who George was. A workmate? He wanted to get them to explain how this solo trip – and he knew that much; it had been confirmed it was supposed to be just Sammy – had converted into a shared holiday, but he didn't know how to raise it.

Had Helen known another person was a possibility and not told him? But that wasn't her style: she was a spreadsheet maker, someone who set up shared calendars.

'Remind me how you two know each other?'

'We went to the same college,' said Sammy. 'But we kind of just recently met.'

'Oh yeah? Whereabouts?'

'Just around,' said Sammy.

'At some kind of event?'

'You could call it that,' said George.

'It definitely was eventful,' said Sammy.

'Like...' Henry's mind grasped, what did Sammy actually do? '... a church thing?'

George looked at Sammy, who looked at George.

'Not exactly,' laughed George.

'But sort of,' said Sammy.

'Huh.' They were both being oddly evasive. 'Is this for some reason top secret?'

'No, no dude, definitely not,' said Sammy locking eyes with George. And they were locked. Henry watched the look linger in his rearview.

'No, not top secret at all,' said George.

'Nope,' said Sammy. 'But you know. It was just a thing.'

By the time they arrived it was after dark. Both boys – men really, but also just boys, bright-eyed, still fresh-faced – had fallen asleep on the backseat, woke only when the car stopped and Henry spoke to tell them they were here.

Between the seats, he saw George softly pat Sammy's knee. 'Sam dude.'

'Yeah?' said Sammy, groggy.

'I think this is it.'

Sammy exhaled, long, and something changed.

'Okay,' he said.

In the lift up to Henry's flat, both of them were silent, snuck looks to each other but mostly stared at the ground as if thinking.

And in that strange way you can feel tension boiling in your body, almost in your breath, in anticipation, even when it's for someone else, Henry knew it was nerves, their nerves. A kind of tightening that tightened again when they opened the door to Helen, who screamed her brother's name, stomped her feet, threw her arms wide open, then stopped dead, frozen: George.

'Sorry,' she said. 'Who's this?'

'Helen, dude, this is George right here.'

'Hey,' said George. 'Pleasure.'

'Who?'

'My pal George from D.C.'

'Your roommate?'

'No, that's *Jim* not George. We *definitely* do not live together.'

'Imagine if we lived together!' said George, but not even Sammy laughed.

'Wait. Who?'

'He's just like.' A long pause. 'This is George, dude.'

Helen shook her head at Henry, mouthed *Who?*, and Henry stepped away to signal he had no idea about anything, really anything to do with any of this at all. No one moved for so long it was obvious no one was moving, so Henry ushered the two guys through, into the living room, said he and Helen would make some tea – to which Sammy said '*Tea!*' – and Henry closed the door to seal them in.

Helen spoke in a fast whisper, switching on the kettle. 'Who the fuck is that White guy?'

'George?'

'Who's George? Why is my brother showing up to visit me in England with my boyfriend with some random... *guy?* I don't know a George. Who's George? And why are they dressed the same? It's weird.'

'They're both dressed like your dad, to be fair.'

Helen snapped her face up at him, four empty mugs in front of her. 'What's Dad got to do with this?'

'You know what I mean.' He paused. 'Sorry.'

She frowned, dropped teabags, shook her head. 'I hate tea. And I don't know why you have to bring Dad into everything.'

'I was just talking about the clothes – the matching clothes.'

'He's my dad. And why's this weird guy in my

house?' said Helen, the kettle boiling. She poured too much water, too little milk, four cups all a very brown brown. She repeated, 'Who is he?' to herself.

Henry was tempted to say 'his friend', but instead just said 'I have no idea.'

'I don't like him.'

'I think—'

'Sammy always used to have these weird little guys he'd bring around. These little guys who followed him everywhere like puppies. Like a new one every year. It was weird. From at least when he started junior high school. Roald, Jensen, I think. *Jace*. They were like these little leech people who were always into weird stuff. His normal friends are fine, but he'd always find this one little guy. I thought he grew out of it.'

'I mean. George seems alright—' said Henry, but she'd already left the kitchen.

In the living room, George was saying to Helen, in the exact same words Sammy had used at the airport, as if they'd rehearsed it, that he could easily get a hotel room. And Sammy said it too, straight after, almost verbatim, effectively confirming that they had practiced.

Helen waved her hand at the suggestion, angry.

'No, Sammy, what? Of course not.'

'But—'

'No,' she said, then interrogated them:

She thought it was just Sammy.

Yeah, but. George really wanted to come and it was just a couple of days here, so.

Were they friends from school?

Yeah more or less.

How long had they been hanging out?

Like a couple years?

Where'd they meet.

At a thing.

What thing?

A thing.

'What thing?'

Henry just watched, a side of Helen he'd never seen revealing itself – less accommodating, more intense; her brother turning her into a stereotypical older sister, overbearing.

Sammy and his stunt double sat next to each other on the couch and, during the onslaught, Helen firing her questions, Henry caught a quick movement from George. Only a flash – a hand on Sammy's knee, squeezing, lifted.

Then he realised.

The way they moved in parallel; sat together in the car at the back as odd as that was; the outfits; the way they kept each other entertained with their conversation about nothing.

They were dating.

One extra friend, Helen said. Following him around. Always one guy. For about a year.

Henry wondered if this was some kind of trial coming out, first to the sister then to the parents with the sister – the test Helen was making him take doubled for her with George. Poor George.

'Sammy. What thing?' Helen asked.

'I don't really think it's a—'

'What thing?'

'Like. A rally.'

This was it.

'A rally for what?'

'I don't think it's that big a deal,' said George, answering for Sammy, as couples do. 'We couldn't not do it. And we didn't know what would happen.'

This was it, thought Henry. How crazy that this is what this trip was going to be.

'What rally?' said Helen.

'For the President.'

'Which President?'

'The last one,' said Sammy, almost apologetically. 'At the Capitol. A couple years back. The big one. For the election.'

Henry gawped. Closed his mouth, opened it. 'Sorry, what?'

George was an organiser, Sammy said with a long sigh. They'd met online after the results came in and it was obvious everything was backwards and people needed to get together and speak up. It was great because he was local, so it was easy to set up a hub for people from the city and from outside of the city to—

'What?' said Henry as Helen shook her head in way that seemed disappointed but not surprised. 'Come on, Sammy...' she said.

'I mean we totally don't condone a lot of what people were doing,' said George, again speaking for them. 'But the statement was like... unequivocal?'

'Totally,' said Sammy smiling.

'Are you coming out to me as a terrorist right now?' Helen said. 'Are you like a Proud Boy?'

'No! No way,' said Sammy.

'I mean those guys definitely have bad elements, but I don't think we should totally dismiss what they've done for our movement,' said George. 'Because the—'

'He needs to get a hotel,' said Helen, short.

'No, but I'm saying,' said George, 'the main problem is that aggression and intimidation tactics don't
win hearts and minds!'

Everyone stopped.

'I meant about the Proud Boys.'

Helen stood up, walked out, slammed the door.

There was a response here that Henry was supposed to make but he didn't know what it was. Chase
Helen? Something specific you say to younger brothers? Throw them both out?

'Is that why you're wearing the same clothes?' he
asked. 'For... the movement?'

'No,' Sammy said. 'There was a sale.'

'Prices were actually pretty decent,' said George.

Helen came back in, arms full of sheets, a duvet
– dumped them. 'He can sleep on the couch tonight.
Sammy, you're in the guest room, it's made up. We
can talk in the morning,' she said and left.

Henry checked his phone to confirm what he
suspected. It was only just past 7.30pm.

'Go to sleep now?' said Sammy.

'Is that like a custom?'

'I'll go talk to her,' Henry said, thought: Families.

In their bedroom, Helen lay face down, perpendicular to the bed itself, her legs hanging off the edge.

Henry told her it was a little too early to sleep, and she said then tell them to go for a walk, anywhere – Jewellery Quarter, Grand Central, Five Ways – she didn't care. This was a disaster.

'This is awful,' she said, her voice muffled by the mattress. 'My brother just told me he's a neo-Nazi. When you're supposed to be hanging out and bonding.'

'I don't think they're neo-Nazis. And I thought you said your brother was amazing.'

She turned around so he could see her face. 'He is amazing. He's also a dumbass.' She shook her head. 'Where the hell does he find these people? And what the hell are we supposed to do with him for the next few days? And *George* – who the hell is *George?*' Then her eyes popped. '*Oh no.*'

What next? Henry thought. What now?

'A pillow,' said Helen. 'I forgot to give him a pillow. I don't want him to think I'm the type of person who doesn't give a guest a pillow.'

He just did what she said. Left the bedroom, having fun imagining Sammy and George walking through central Birmingham tonight and pointing at everything, what they would make of it, what everyone would make of them. He had the feeling that this would be all the fun he'd be having until Sammy left.

Families, he thought, pillow in hand, and cracked the door to the living room, stopping abruptly when he heard Sammy's voice on the other side:

'That was really bad. I was kind of hoping we could've avoided that.'

'Well. At least now she knows,' said George. 'It'll be alright, dude. Really. She'll get used to it. We can tell her the rest tomorrow.'

Henry waited for them to go quiet, then pushed the door open to the two of them, paralleled: sitting shoulder to shoulder, in Oxford shirts and pleated chinos, one with glasses, one without, briefly kissing.

White Wedding

1.

The first problem was the Botox. The goal had been for the bride to get a small touch just above her left eyebrow which, in times of crisis, had the tendency to betray her with a tic. Unfortunately, a dog had just been at the salon an hour before she arrived. The woman administering the shot did the eyebrow fine, but suggested perhaps one further dose above the bridge of the nose; you know, preventatively. The bride said yes, fixed her face, then sneezed the whole needle to the hilt into her tear duct. She returned home, six hours later, to the flat she shared with the groom, the whole of the left side of her head frozen, immobile, drooping and baby-skin smooth. You could wear a mask? he suggested.

2.

The second problem was the best man, Stanley. He'd been instructed by email, text message and several face-to-face pub conversations that certain topics were off limits for his speech:

a) He was not to tell the truth about how the bride and groom first met at a sex party organised by the Free Love Society at their university. He was not to say, especially, that he met the bride there first, then the groom, and that fluids had been exchanged between the three of them, in combinations none could remember because, as they found out afterwards, the FLS spiked both the food and the drinks at all their events with any drug they could find.

b) He was not to talk about the groom's feet, which were massive, hooknailed, atrocious things that he had worked hard to hide from the bride's family and friends for five years, at all costs, pursuing wild and contortionate stratagems to shield them at beach parties, on holidays, and after getting rain-soaked several times to the bone. The best man, Stanley, had said he would be respectful of the groom's feet but he had a good riff he'd thunk up about different things he could compare them to: toes like pizza crusts, nails like sausage skins, and things like that. All foodstuffs the bride and groom, as vegans, didn't eat, he said – and he'd weave that into comments about their veganism, how it's trendy now, something about quinoa, and then spin that out into something endearing about how he loved them both and wished them well. That was kind of his outline. No, definitely not, the groom said, because

c) He was not to talk about veganism. It was simple; the subject was touchy with family at the best of times. The groom's father had had a 26-hour row with him spread across two weeks and six days about serving vegan food only at the reception, during the course of which the groom's father called vegans A SCIENTOLOGY-LIKE CULT, A BUNCH OF PSYCHOPATHIC BASTARDS, and DEONTOLOGISTS!, the last insult giving them both pause and leading to a mutually agreed termination of the argument so both could rest and take stock. Veganism, said the groom, is an ethical lifestyle, but one predicated (he said that, 'predicated', and Stanley took out his phone, opened Notes, and typed it, 'predicated' and, as an aide memoire, 'always talks funny') on an implicit denunciation of the way that others lived. The bride, said the groom, was always offended by his veganism for that reason when they met; at that time she believed in live and let live, but after watching some videos of abattoirs with him, on date seven or so, she was swayed. In general, he said, unless they were soulless, people knew that eating meat was evil. That's why chicken nuggets exist, he said definitively; didn't explain, cracked his knuckles, and ended, So no veganism.

3.

The third problem was the bride and groom's parents, who hated each other. All of them. Both sets of parents hated their own partners, and each individual hated all the others. When they met, crisscrossed lines of hatred sliced the room into mini-fiefdoms; and, as a result, the bride and groom tried to stand or sit between each potential pairing simultaneously, and so stood up and sat down quite a lot. It was tiring. The bride's parents had been divorced in all but law since she was thirteen, while the groom's parents were generally resentful of everything, not least each other, as a scam of capitalism. Thus when the bride's father put forward his draft budget of £30,000 for the

wedding in the couples' second meeting, the groom's
father stood up from the couch, raised his hand aloft
and declaimed, in summary, Marx's 'The Fetishism of
the Commodity and Its Secret'. The bride's mother,
in response, asked if the groom wanted to wear a tra-
ditional suit. Both fathers tutted, and then the bride's
father asked the groom's father what, specifically,
made him think he could talk like that to his wife.
I didn't talk, he said, I scoffed. The groom's mother
took that chance to lean back on the couch, cross her
legs, and say, with a dismissive swipe of her hand, that
the impending and necessary total economic collapse
meant that they might as well blow all their savings
on a wedding that would, let's be honest with each
other, probably fail in a year or so unless the bride
got pregnant which would (she said this part con-
spiratorially to the bride's mother) as we know, only
prolong the agony of being shackled to a man in a
relationship of dominance and subjection predicated
on the perpetuation of systems of heteropatriarchal,
phallogocentripetal force; this while the two men
stepped across the room to each other, the polo shirt
and khaki shorts of the one silently wailing at the flak
jacket and fatigues of the other. Under no circum-
stances would the groom's mother wear a dress, the
groom's father make small talk with the bourgeoisie,

the bride's father shake hands with that twat, and the bride's mother not wear pink. Those were the rules of engagement.

4.

The fourth problem was the groom's penis, which stopped working at 15:30 on Saturday the 6th of May, one week before the wedding. It was an average penis in all ways; in fact, one of the attractions of the Free Love Society's Autumn Sex Jam was what the groom then saw as an opportunity to, if he couldn't stretch the thing (he'd tried) or widen it (he'd known of no way to even think of how to do this), at least learn to have sex from sunset to sunrise without a break. The tactic didn't work, in no small part because he didn't last long in the club, attending only the inaugural Sex Jam and remembering nothing other than arriving at the venue, drinking a sparkling water then waking up next to the bride in a pile on the carpet and instantly falling in love with her, forever. He proposed to her then, for the first of four times, but she was asleep. He shook her awake and, losing his nerve in the light of her eyes – eyes, despite his BA and MA he still couldn't describe – instead asked her if she wanted to leave and get a coffee. She said no, but he could call her. His penis, then, was a virile and active weasel which only rarely let him down. His penis (which after seeing some film he was calling 'The Irradiator', for a short while, in drunken conversations with friends, which now included the future best man, Stanley) loved the bride and her body, her exhalations and mannerisms, her hairsmell and her charms, and it was happy to engage with her whenever either he, the groom, or the bride asked for its attention. Then that Saturday it just broke.

He said then, *Ah, man.*

They had decided in advance of the wedding to abstain from sex for a full month in order to make the wedding night and honeymoon interesting. She hadn't asked but he'd taken upon himself the heavy challenge of also abstaining from his morning session of self-love in the shower. That challenge was far greater than he could have ever conceived it to be, his penis becoming some wild Grecian deity in his jeans, storming at every mild provocation and threatening to enter the world of men and set things right. After one week the groom found himself attracted to things that weren't attractive: women's elbows and knees, dresses' seams, chips of dandruff dusted on the shoulders of coats. He went wild, advertisements on everything beaming cleavage at him, women everywhere reeking of something he could only describe as 'woman', his waking mind obsessed with combinations, permutations, his breath always shallow and heavy. Living with the bride became too much – her body was everywhere, literally; she was sometimes naked; often she wore tight clothes.

On Saturday when the bride left for another dress-fitting, he found himself on his knees burying his face into a ravel of her gym stuff, huffing nosefuls of her odour, stuffing his head up into the waistband of her yoga shorts, and then went, that day, actually insane. He leapt to his feet, shorts covering his ears, and howled; circled their small flat on all fours yipping, bounding from surface to surface beating his chest, slamming his forehead on the cushions of their couch. He couldn't wait, fired up the internet on his computer, typed 'bums' and lost the next two hours in shame. When he returned to himself, he looked down at his lap and laptop screen in horror; in part because of the mess and in part because his penis remained erect even though he was not, in any way, aroused.

It took a further two hours to confirm that something was wrong; a further two days – five days left before the wedding, a spell of time in which he had to enlist the aid of one of the tiny belts the bride often wore below her ribcage to strap himself to his own thigh and out of sight – to establish that the erection was – to all intents and purposes, beyond the bounds of the best internet science and the doctor at the Walk-In clinic, who, unable to help herself, guffawed in the middle of his story ('Ahem. I'm really sorry about that. Go on.') – permanent. He now had a hitchhiker's thumb forever thrusting out below his waistband, or at least until the tests came back in two weeks.

5., 6.,7.,8.,9.

There were other problems. Cousin Benjamin who was always high. The maid of honour, Marion, who didn't think the joke about her name and her role was funny at all and threatened to stab someone – after actually breaking a bottle, sweeping all of the pints and glasses off a table, and kicking the same table over – if she heard it one more time at the pre-wedding drinks. A family of ducks lived in the church. Three men who lived near the reception venue who had seen the film *The Wedding Crashers* were determined to re-enact it but dressed as zombies. And it was supposed to be overcast.

10.

The wedding took place on a sunny Saturday, the 13th of May, at 14:00 in Saint Paul's Anglican Church. The bride sipped drinks from a straw stuck in the right side of her mouth. In the best man's speech, Stanley said 'predicated on a sex party' seven times. The groom's father grabbed the DJ's microphone and read selections from 'Reification and the Consciousness of the Proletariat' by György Lukács. Cousin Benjamin was high, Marion thumped someone in the women's bathroom and broke her jaw, a family of ducks lived in the church, and three zombies were turned away at the door. When the dancing started, a small belt slid out of the groom's trouser cuff to hula hoop around his ankle, but no one noticed his erection.

The Mature Student

He'd sit in the back corner and when people said things he didn't like he'd shake his head and say *Jesus!* The seminar leader couldn't have been older than twenty-nine, had a lot of curly brown hair, unusually large eyes, and didn't know what to do with him. She'd offer opportunities, pitch things at him like, 'Angus, could you tell us more about that?' and he'd go into a little tizzy, flop back into his chair, cross his arms, tap a foot on the floor, frown his brow like a Klingon, free a hand, squeeze a fist, drop the fist, and go, 'Well, I just don't agree with it!' and then say nothing else at all until the next disagreement:

Jesus!

It was *Howl* that week and Emilia had just said that she'd been carried away by the lilting rhythms of Ginsberg's poetic voice. She, like everyone else, was fresh from A-levels and Angus was at least fifty.

Arg! he added.

'Angus,' the tutor said. 'Can you unpick that for us please?'

It was winter and he was wearing a pink jumper pocked with grey bobbles and the nails on his hands were freshly cut, something clear because he'd just thrust fingers skyward as if on stage and clutching Yorick's skull.

'The thing is,' he started, then dropped his Hamlet hand, shook his head, crossed his arms. 'I just don't *agree* with it.'

'Can you expand further on that please, Angus?' the tutor said, pressing for a change.

He frowned, stared down at his desk, and his notes, and paged through the latter for at least fifteen minutes. In the room were ten other people, including the tutor – all women, except for Charlie, who looked like a baby ferret.

'The problem is,' Angus began. 'It's, well,' he continued, four people tilting forwards in their seats to listen to him; Emilia already shaking her head; the tutor's eyes so wide and bright it was chilling. 'It's just not *realistic*, is it?' he said; was spent, threw himself back in his chair and exhaled.

'*Okay,*' said the tutor, her eyes unblinked. 'Okay. Can anyone else pick up on that? Or should we just move on?'

III

Saint Sebastian

I was having a crisis of representation. I told my wife that and she said she felt it was normal, but in her own way: She said the whole point and problem with everything nowadays was that nobody knew how to say what they wanted to say; that that was the reason why pretty much the whole world was going the way that it was. I told her I felt that sounded too much like the kind of thing a sixteen-year-old blogger might write, like *If only people could say what they meant!* and then the kid would hashtag it or something and maybe one person would read it and then it would be forgotten. 'Exactly,' my wife said, and it took me ten minutes to understand what she meant.

These are the facts: 1) I am a person, 2) I work in a place I don't want to work, 3) I want to write, to be a writer. The central conflict of this story stems, in part, from all of this.

Mounts the Cross

When I was thirteen and he was six my younger brother, Alan, was hit by a car. The gap between us was because my father didn't want kids, argued with my mom about it for years before he gave in, then got depressed when having me was really hard. Sometime after I was born my dad declared that that was it, and my mom agreed, said fine, until, and no one admits they know why, Alan appeared. My father took years to come to terms with it, in part, apparently, because Alan looked nothing like him. And then a guy named Mike Marriott hit Alan with his car. I didn't see it, but if you've watched enough movies you can work out what it was like. A six-year-old kid, a car with a driver changing radio stations and going fifty-five on a residential street, a bouncing blue ball bouncing in front of him, he hits his brakes, too late.

I often wake up in the middle of the night sweating, with an idea in my head. Just yesterday I flew forward and pushed my hand through everything on the nightstand and knocked it all down. My wife grumbled and I rolled out of bed, questing around our flat for a pen – *A pen! My kingdom for a pen!* But, like a nightmare, there was somehow not one single pen anywhere in our apartment. Not anywhere, or at least not anywhere I could see in the dark, with my glasses off, in a gloom with an insistent idea in my brain – a dream idea, an angry idea, something that felt right. There was a pencil I found, on the kitchen countertop, but I wanted a pen, *a pen!*, and when I made that decision, when I thought *This pencil is not a pen!* the idea was gone. Something about a man who gets a face transplant that his body rejects and that story saying something meaningful about identity, the twenty-first century, about meaning, loss and capitalism but in a real moving way that somebody could read and think *I've never looked at things like that,* but of course, the idea was gone.

My dad went crazy after my brother passed away. Not immediately; he simmered first then started hissing and spitting before he boiled. He started sleeping with anyone and everyone he could, drinking – middle-aged man on a rampage stuff and my mom kept forgiving him for all of it until she realised that, in fact, he didn't want to be forgiven. They didn't divorce though, my parents. Instead with me Mom got more and more confessional, strange, telling me things I never wanted to know at odd times when I couldn't escape. She said things like 'I'm still a woman, whatever your father thinks,' and left me to connect the dots. On a Monday morning once before I left for school, she said the one thing no one ever taught her was who to marry. People tell you where and when to have sex; what kind of men to avoid altogether; they say at what stage in your life you should think about settling down, but never how and who to marry, and then, once you're married, how not to get it wrong.

S tories about writers are boring because writers are, effectively, professional masturbators. If they're lucky, people pay to look at what their masturbation makes, but, more often, they just masturbate for their own sake. That's why in movies about writers they keep actual scenes of fingers on keys or gripping pen and pencil shafts to the minimum. No one wants to watch that. We want to see the products, the fictions, the poems, the plays, the overdoses, the obscenity trials, Sean Connery; we don't want to see someone alone in a room looking angrily off at nothing, working out the best verb to use, getting grumpy about adjectives, jealous of other authors' successes and reading rejection emails. How do you film a whole wasted day on Twitter, the agonising decision whether or not to change out of your pyjamas? I tell my wife this, and she groans. 'Writers write,' she says. 'You're not writing.' 'I have to think about the industry,' I say. 'They don't want me. Everything I try, nobody wants it.' 'I have faith,' she says. 'But they all just want something straight.' 'Then write something straight.'

My mother started sleeping with a guy named Abel Mainer, who was ex-Amish (however that worked) but still had a perimeter beard. He was gentle, she said, and I didn't want to know. My dad, we thought, was at this time sleeping with the C.O.O. at his work, and we knew this or thought this because she kept leaving him answering machine messages when she had no reason to about 'something just came up.' 'She's shameless,' my mother said, and I actually agreed with her out loud, but then I found out about Abel Mainer, who I called 'Honest Abe' to her face because I was eighteen, almost done with school and just feeling like I had to get out of that house. 'Not honest,' she said. 'More gentle.' And I groaned.

I read in a book by John Gardner that all writers write because they have a wound, *like some fatal childhood accident for which one feels fully responsible and can never fully forgive oneself. It is the pain of the wound which impels the artist to do his work, and it is the universality of woundedness in the human condition which makes the work of art significant as medicine or distraction.* I've never talked to anyone about this but it's hard to argue with, I guess at least for me. My wife says I should write something truthful, to stop hiding, to stop dressing up my own grief. I argue, say that's writing – everyone is trying to disguise their autobiography; it's like that masturbation analogy I made the other day. But she's right. Like Hemingway said, if he really said it, *There's nothing to writing. All you do is sit at a typewriter and bleed.* So bleed.

Right after my brother died was the closest my family ever got. We were united in loss, I guess, and no one could question how we felt. An undeniable tragedy: you don't get that too often in life and it makes you feel righteous. At school, kids who hadn't ever seemed to see me now at least looked, teachers pulled me aside, my friends tip-toed around any mention of Alan. It took me and my mother longer to realise than my dad what freedom other people's sympathy gave us. Dad at work, some forty-year-old lady flies in from out of town, both of them wearing wedding rings and he invites her out for an after-work drink. They sit together at a booth in the back corner of a sports bar, he tells a pretty good joke. She's wide-eyed, energetic, unlike my mom at home. All he has to say is 'I've just lost my son' and then all bets are off: he can ask her if she wants another, he can touch her accidentally on purpose all night long, they can kiss and keep on kissing. 'I've just lost my son,' he can say when she pulls away, says they shouldn't. 'My son,' he can say. 'My son.'

My mother is with Honest Abe; my father is with at least the C.O.O. and talks about buying a boat like it's the most logical next step; and I go off to college. They both drive me to up Gainesville and the whole way there they're talking in this fake tone and everything is too much and everything is strange. My dad then says some nonsense about how it's good my dorm is near a fire station, and we all laugh about it because it doesn't make sense. This is the thickest and sharpest cheese of a family moment and I think we all know it, but we all want it so bad, and my dad even holds my mom's hand when we get out of the car. We go inside the dorm and unpack, and my mom can't help herself. She says, sitting down on my soon-to-be roommate's bed, 'I think we should all talk.' And we do try, almost, but we don't really want to, we just want to be in this, as it is. So Mom says, 'It's gonna be hard,' and Dad says, 'You better hope your roommate doesn't have b.o.' and we all laugh again and abandon it. Dad leaves first, to smoke, and my mom lingers, looking at my stuff; I don't have that much stuff. 'It'll be good,' she says. 'You'll enjoy this.' 'And you and Dad?' 'We'll be fine. We'll find our way.' 'Mom,' I tell her, because I don't want her to go just yet. 'I think I want to write about what happened, with Alan.' 'Okay,' she says, distracted. 'Do what you want. Just don't write about us.'

I spend afternoons and evenings reading about writers, thinking about writing. I find interviews, order books by people I admire but just make a mountain of them by our bedside. I dream of acceptance speeches, advances, tell my wife my theories about everything. I try writing a story about a tech company in the future that makes a device that lets you spy on your friends. I try writing a story about a girl stuck in a dead-end job. I read stories by Lorrie Moore, Jhumpa Lahiri, get depressed. In his essay 'Postmodernism, or the Cultural Logic of Late Capitalism', Fredric Jameson says that all culture is, now, commodified; everything dances to the rhythm of markets, the preeminent cultural form is flat, depthless, self-referential, speaking only to and at itself. 'So what?' says my wife. 'So everything eats itself – nothing touches meaning or morality or transcends the immediate – nothing instructs, informs, elevates.' 'So you're telling me the reason you can't finish your story... (she's washing dishes) is because of capitalism?' 'Yes.' 'Just write something straight,' she tells me. 'Just try. Just try as hard as you can and write something true.' 'But I don't know what's true.' 'Then just write that.'

roads

All he could think when he saw the bodies was that everyone was going to get sick. How couldn't they? Bodies pressed into and over each other and so close they blended into one single thing, broken only by banners, by slogans, STOP KILLING BLACK PEOPLE SAY HIS NAME WE WILL NOT BE SILENT They'd get sick. LOVE BLACK LIVES THE WAY YOU LOVE BLACK CULTURE RACISM IS A PANDEMIC THE UK IS NOT INNOCENT They'd get sick. And then that actor, from the new *Star Wars*, working himself into tears and speaking with a passion undermined by clichés, pleading: *Respect Black women. Black Lives have always mattered. We have always been important.* Then everyone sharing the video he didn't want to see: the knee on the neck – eight minutes, nine minutes, whatever it was – the life crushed out of this guy in broad daylight as, he knew, everyone knew, he cried out for his mother. Mama. He watched the comedian in America who named his set after the exact amount of time it took for the guy to die – not one real joke in the whole thing. He saw the protests: in Germany, in Italy, in New Zealand, in the Netherlands, in Canada, in Sudan and Israel and Denmark. He heard the names, the incantations of names – *Say their names!* – some names you'd catch just once – *Say their names!* —; some names you'd hear again and again and all he could think, and he felt ashamed by it, was They'll get sick. They'll get sick and then they'll say You see them, they get sick. They get too angry. They get worked up. They get sick. They make themselves sick. The reason we're sick is because they're sick. They get sick and make us sick. And that would be the end of it, and then—

His son cried out. That then, whenever was then, all the times that had been then – all the days just one day now; all the nights just one night – when his son cried the only thing there was space for, the only thing the whole world was was the fact that his son was crying, that again he was crying, that again he couldn't sleep. But when the father's mind found a moment, sometimes many hours later, to reopen, he thought They'll get sick. They'll get sick. Please God just don't get sick. Please God just get through this.

He creeps out of bed now, in his boxer shorts. Brushes his teeth as his son keeps crying, moves slowly to the boy's bedroom, blacked out, white noise machine rushing, and the kid stops crying immediately.

Awake! he says.

You're awake, the father says, rubbing his eyes.

Awake! Me!

Not Daddy, the father says, through a yawn.

The boy waits, then, Yeah! he says. Daddy awake!

Am I?

Awake!

It's five am, 5:05, which is better than his wake time yesterday but worse than last week, and much better than when he was a baby. He often thinks like this now, the father: the food thrown on the floor was less than last month's, getting into the bath is better now than it ever was even though he always runs away. The boy knows colours, which is good for his age, can count to three, but often confuses white and yellow and says One Two One Three!

Toast, he says now. Toast. Toast. Want toast.

Is someone hungry?

Me!

Coming right up.

The boy laughs. Won't stop laughing.

The father smiles. Is that funny? Coming right up?

Yeah, he says, still laughing. Daddy funny.

Hilarious.

He laughs harder. No Daddy, *funny*.

At the beginning of this he sent a lot of out-of-the-blue messages – DMs to people he'd been Following or Friends with but who he hadn't exchanged real words with in years. He made the effort to properly reconnect with them, wrote to exes apologetically, saying that he was Sorry and it was strange but everything was strange now and were they okay, were their families alright? He always wondered when he wrote if they'd just ignore him, but they rarely did, which triggered more thinking – did they think of him as often as he thought of them, were there the same aches? regrets? – but he couldn't type that, obviously, and after the initial relieved exchanges, the efforts to rekindle old jokes and dive into a shared past that was always there but also always not, the relationships – with the exes, with the distant friends – returned to their old steady state of silence and distanced watching.

Every morning, the routine is smoother for the two of them, both more comfortable in their new roles: shared breakfast, ten minutes of the kid around and around on the carpet with his toys while his father runs the bath, the television on to the news and the boy practicing all the names he has for things – car! floor! me! – while on screen protests, brushfires, bodies, hurricanes, police cars slammed into teenagers holding only signs for protection and politicians at mics, at lecterns, clenching their fists in that half-clench they think signals strength, but doesn't, and his son says:

Bath Daddy? No Daddy. No!

He's in a WhatsApp group of old university friends called *Is it?*, which until this year was a place for memes, arranging meet-ups, and sharing the occasional baby picture, but then turned, at first, into a space to check in and express hope and concern, then turned further, opening out into what it is now: something like a second, tighter, and more painful Twitter feed. Links to newspaper articles and thinkpieces. Recommendations of books to read and quotations from James Baldwin and Toni Morrison. His White friends on it have slowly gone silent, and he doesn't know if it's because they don't like it, feel they can't comment on it, or something worse; except for their posts elsewhere he wouldn't even know they're all still alive.

After he drops his son off at nursery, he has a half hour before he has to log on for work – just enough time to not know what to do with then lose in his phone, then he's sitting still for the rest of the day, walks at most twenty steps.

On *Is it?* yesterday someone posted a link to an opinion piece and quoted from it: 'slavery and empire are two quite different things', the general gist of the article that empire was good and slavery was abolished and that was it. End of. His friends on the group wrote 'bullshit' 'wtf' 'lol' 'smh'. The father added his own comment, he can't even remember it, only remembers tapping through to see the byline and author picture and knowing before reading it was by the kind of guy whose sole job it is to write that same article in different ways each month.

But still, on Twitter today, in one of the two windows he keeps open for non-work, there's an unfolding scroll of people arguing about the article, attacking and defending the author and the place it was published, and he's addicted – to this thing that happens whenever things like this happen. He doesn't add to it, but can't stop reading and watching because – this always happens too – the thread shifts into debates about, variously, structures, whiteness, Churchill.

It's a bad thing for cultures to mix

This is literally why Winston Churchill said 'If you're going through hell, keep going' 😬

To improve is to change, to be perfect is to change often – Winston Churchill

Why are you campaigning for white-washing and cultural amnesia??

This would be funnier if it wasn't so pathetic

In his other non-work window, he has a web app of picture updates from his son's nursery. They're painting today and the kid's got red paint on his face, red paint on his new grey joggers. They just got those.

On Twitter someone writes I'm a black man and I love Mr Churchill you lot NEED TO GROW UP!!!! Three people write about how other people need to get out of their echo chamber. A colleague emails URGENT, and then the day is over, was always over, and the father collects his son.

The same bubbly nursery lady greets him every Monday, Tuesday and Thursday evening. She's dressed in the same purple tunic they all wear, the corporate nursery logo stitched over her heart. He knows her name but never feels he knows her well enough to use it, to even enter into the kind of conversation where you might need a name, even though she, and others who he also never refers to by name, have been looking after his son five days a week for the better part of a year.

She's over-bright, the lady – bursting, he'd describe her as; speaks in that high, soft, slow and excited way that young kids seem to like, but his son is ambivalent about, and greets the father, as 'Dad', as in: *Hi Dad!* She hands over his son and in her eyes he sees a question about why it's been him – for the last four weeks, five, only ever the father at drop off and pick up, never the mother, not once.

'He's been brilliant,' she says. 'He's had a very very good day.'

> Had you asked the father what fatherhood would be like before he became a father, he would have said it would be hard. Fathering without any clear sense of what it meant, when you'd dreamt what you'd be in life was something very different, something else. Fathering now, in this world, as it was, where it was going. He mainly cast his imagination forward back when his wife was pregnant; imagined himself with a much

older child, not a baby or a toddler, and that child doting on him. Most often when he imagined them together, him and his son – it had to be a son; he knew it would be a son – he would see the kid trailing him, the two of them walking into the city centre, rounding the corner from their flat toward the world. In those dreams the kid would be perfectly content in his father's presence but always faceless, faceless but obviously happy. How he could tell he was happy the father doesn't know. But he was. Had to be. And yet still, he'd think, This is going to be too hard. I don't know if I can do this.

Online everyone's still writing about Churchill. They've boarded up a statue of him to protect against vandalism and a group of NF or BNP or EDL or whatever they are now members are trying to organise 24-hour protection. They have one of them on BBC News in a clip everyone's circulating saying the way some people are treating our country is a disgrace. Someone remixes it to a drill beat. Someone posts a fake video of the remix. Someone Rick Rolls it. Someone writes a thinkpiece about how the Rick Roll is nostalgic callback to the pre-pandemic era. Someone adds a post about that to *Is it?*. On *Is it?* someone writes 'wtf'. The father ends up lost in an autoplay of videos on YouTube that night, ends with one called STATUES OF SLAVEHOLDERS YOU DIDN'T KNOW YOU WERE SEEING, someone posting in the comments 'all images of ENSLAVERS show the West is no home for us, never will be', someone else writing 'who should we make statues of then, slaves?', someone else writing 'most of those people achieved more in life than you ever will', someone else writing 'And probably you too'.

On the weekends he takes his son for long walks; both on foot for as long as his son can manage, then the boy lifted into his pushchair and wheeled with the pace picked up. There are so many beautiful parts of this city, places the father didn't even know existed, wouldn't have seen if not for this – the Vale, Cannon Hill, Lickey Hills.

Tree! his son says. Car! Crane! Van! Dada – van!

He can't, the father, remember what it was like to be a boy. Most of his memories are so merged with images from photo albums he's not sure anymore if they even count as memories. So far as he has anything, he has his feelings – of warmth with his parents, of joy when he rode his bike, of fear in the cinema when someone – and he doesn't know whose idea it was but his own father was there – took him to see a horror film too young. It all seems soaked in sepia, his childhood, a past too perfect when everything online says there was no perfect past, that the only hope comes after now.

Dada! Birds! Car!

He read, when his son was young and he'd read anything, everything, to give him advice on what to do, a blog that said the biggest challenge a new parent faced was to feel the joy and awe for your children when they're awake that you feel when you see them asleep. He didn't get that initially but now he does; he does feel it – both joy and awe – not always, but in moments that swell up in him out of nowhere, out of air. It's what he feels about himself as a child, awe at the impossibility of that time – that state of being suspended untouched by the world, until you are.

At drop off it's the same lady, the ginger one with the voice, whose eyes hold questions she never asks and he never answers.

'*Good morning, you!* Any messages, Dad?' she asks, her eyebrows raised above her mask, her red hair roughly ponytailed, loose hairs springing. Her accent is Midlandsish, her height is average. There are pictures of her without a mask on the nursery website but in real life he's never seen the bottom half of her face.

Early on, very early on, when his son just started here, after the confirmation that because of his wife's job he could attend, the father got a sense that this woman didn't like him or his son, and he told his wife, 'I don't know. I don't know.'

'You think she's racist? He's just a baby.'

'I dunno,' the father said. 'I just want him to be treated the same way as the other children.'

'He will be,' his wife said. Then she didn't speak for a very long time before she said, like an echo, at the dropped volume of an echo, 'He will be.'

And she was fine, the woman, overall, as fine as anyone else with the boy – he was cute, he won most people over, but with the father himself it was different, felt different.

'No, no messages,' he says.

He's thought a lot about the coming conversation, wondered when it will happen, how:

Are we—? his son would say, or

Someone at school called me—, or

Because we're … does that mean we…

And he doesn't know what to say, what he could say. He thinks about it always, the fact of it always waiting. Once, having walked through trees and streets, happily – whenever it is, was – standing with his son outside of a hotel to take a second to catch his breath, their walk good – plenty of things for the kid to see – the father spotted a statue of a man he'd never noticed cemented there: the statue's stone eyes on the horizon, arms spread, two women draped at his feet. The plaque below the man read HE LABOURED TO BRING FREEDOM TO THE NEGRO SLAVE THE VOTE TO BRITISH WORKMEN AND THE PROMISE OF PEACE TO A WAR-WORN WORLD

Man! his son said. Man there! And lady. Two! Two lady!

And what will he say, the father? What will he say?

What will I say?

Like everyone he wonders a lot now about dying, about what it would be like to die: gulping and grasping but never enough air; your lungs compressed by this thing with a name that doesn't capture at all what it does to you. What does it feel like in that moment to see the last faces you'll ever see, and hear, or not –

their words? This body that so long carried you, held you, that was you, now not yours at all, taken.

And he thinks, the father, his mind filled with images of his son: I can't. I can't go. I have to survive. And in those times, whenever those times are, in those moments that are always, including now, he thinks of slogans STOP KILLING BLACK PEOPLE SAY HIS NAME WE WILL NOT BE SILENT LOVE BLACK LIVES THE WAY YOU LOVE BLACK CULTURE RACISM IS A PANDEMIC THE UK IS NOT INNOCENT sees bodies pressed into and over each other so close they blend into one single thing – all they are made into one single thing.

And his son cries out.

And he checks the time.

And in the boy's room. In his boxer shorts. The father rubs his eyes.

Awake, Daddy. Dada.

Awake.

NOTES

'Limbs' was first published on the Galley Beggar Press website after being shortlisted for their short story prize.

'Mirrors' was originally a commission for the West Midlands Readers' Network.

An earlier version of 'roads' was a commission for Lincoln University and read live in draft form on 28 October 2021.

The quotes on page 100 are taken from John Gardner, *On Becoming a Novelist* (New York: W. W. Norton, 1983), p. 62; and John Gardner, *On Moral Fiction* (New York: Basic Books, 1978), p. 181.

Thank you to everyone who has encouraged and supported my fiction writing, including and especially Arathi Papineni McIntosh, Kavita Bhanot, Jane Commane, Andrew Cowan, Jonathan Davidson, and Emma Dai'an Wright. Thanks also, for help with this book, to Mike Browning, Neela Doležalová, Rachel Forisha, and Emily Slater.

ABOUT THE AUTHOR

Malachi McIntosh was born in Birmingham, England, but grew up in the United States. His fiction and non-fiction have been published in *The Caribbean Review of Books*, the *Guardian*, the *Independent*, and Comma Press's *Book of Birmingham*.

He is the recipient of a British Library Eccles Fellowship and a Royal Society of Literature Giles St Aubyn Award. His stories have been shortlisted for multiple prizes and commissioned by the National Trust and Lincoln University.

Malachi was Editor and Publishing Director of *Wasafiri* from 2019-2022 and currently teaches English at Oxford University. *Parables, Fables, Nightmares* is his first collection.

Tiny Moons

Nina Mingya Powles

Tiny Moons is a collection of essays about food and belonging. Nina Mingya Powles journeys between Wellington, Kota Kinabalu and Shanghai, tracing the constants in her life: eating and cooking, and the dishes that have come to define her.

Through childhood snacks, family feasts, Shanghai street food and student dinners, she attempts to find a way back towards her Chinese-Malaysian heritage.

'Meditative reflections on family, solitude, and belonging, intertwined with mouthwatering descriptions of noodles, dumplings, and sesame pancakes.' *Book Riot*

'Funny, compact and beautifully written.' *New Statesman*

PAPERBACK ISBN 978-1-912915-34-7

PRICE £8.99

How Kyoto Breaks Your Heart

Florentyna Leow

20-something and uncertain about her future, Florentyna Leow is exhilarated when an old acquaintance offers her an opportunity for work and cohabitation in a little house in the hills of Kyoto.

Florentyna begins a new job as a tour guide, taking tourists on elaborate and expensive trips around Kyoto's cultural hotspots. Meanwhile, her relationship with her new companion develops an intensity as they live and work together. Their relationship burns bright, but seasons change, the persimmon tree out back loses its fruit, and things grow strange between the two women.

PAPERBACK ISBN 9781915628008

PRICE £8.99

Night-time Stories

Edited by Yen-Yen Lu

A child waits for the tooth fairy; a mother spends a night watching a recording of the previous night; two women face the ghosts that haunted their grandmothers. The nights in these ten stories are thick and substantial, ambiguous and alluring.

Eerie, magical, hushed and surprisingly alive, this anthology shows the night as a place where connections are made and daylit lives can be changed.

With stories from Valentine Carter, John Kitchen, Winifred Mok, Leanne Radojkovich, Angela Readman, Jane Roberts, Rebecca Rouillard, Miyuki Tatsuma, Zoë Wells and Sofija Ana Zovko.

PAPERBACK ISBN 978-1-912915-60-6
PRICE £8.99

ABOUT THE EMMA PRESS

small press, big dreams

୦୫ଞ୦

The Emma Press is an independent publishing house based in the Jewellery Quarter, Birmingham, UK. It was founded in 2012 by Emma Dai'an Wright and specialises in poetry, short fiction and children's books. In 2020 The Emma Press received funding from Arts Council England's Elevate programme, developed to enhance the diversity of the arts and cultural sector by strengthening the resilience of diverse-led organisations.

The Emma Press is passionate about publishing literature which is welcoming and accessible. Visit our website and find out more about our books here:

Website: theemmapress.com
Facebook @theemmapress
Twitter @theemmapress
Instagram @theemmapress

CONTENTS